Acoustical Perspective on Raga-Rasa Theory

Rasa, as an aesthetic experience, has always been a dominant feature of art and art criticism in India. This study examines *rasa* as related to Indian music, specially the *raga*. A new approach has been made for understanding the complex issue of *raga-rasa* relation, wherein, theories and tools of modern scientific technology have been employed. This may perhaps be the first work in recent times to examine the aspects of intonation and melodic movement in the actual performance context, using very sensitive computer software.

A specially innovative section of the book deals with a detailed comparison between Indian and Western viewpoints on the issue of music and emotion. The exhaustive literature survey presented on the subject of *raga-rasa* provides excellent source material on the subject. It includes the historical evolution of *rasa* as applied to various aspects of Indian music. Although no specificity in terms of a particular *rasa* can be attached to the aesthetic experience associated with a *raga*, this study reassures that the principles inherent in a *raga* and their aesthetic capabilities are not mere theoretical norms but a reality leading to the blissful experience of *rasa*.

Dr. Suvarnalata Srinivasa Rao is presently a research scientist and co-ordinator (music) at the National Centre for the Performing Arts, Bombay. An accomplished sitar-performer, she is the disciple of Pandit Arvind Parikh. Dr. Rao has been a visiting faculty for various institutions at home and abroad.

A recipient of many national and international fellowship. Dr. Rao has a number of presentations and publications to her credit including several research papers and the forthcoming volume entitled "Raga Guide". Recently, she has been awarded the prestigious Homi Bhabha Fellowship for undertaking research on "Instrument making".

Acoustical Perspective on Raga-Rasa Theory

Suvarnalata Rao

Munshiram Manoharlal
Publishers Pvt. Ltd.

ISBN 81-215-0878-9
First published 2000

Typeset, printed and published by
Munshiram Manoharlal Publishers Pvt. Ltd.,
Post Box 5715, 54 Rani Jhansi Road, New Delhi 110 055.

Contents

Preface

The beginning of scientific and experimental methodology in India can be found as early as 200 BC in the works on Music. Bharata's *Natyashastra* dating back to this period bears testimony to this fact. However, thereafter the concepts proposed herein and in similar works have never been reviewed in the context of contemporary performance practices.

In recent times, Bharata's formulations regarding *jati-rasa* and the *raga-rasa* relation resulting from it, have been met with criticism. Different approaches have been adopted by some of the modern musicologists to restate the *rasa*-theory in the context of contemporary performing practice of *raga*. Having the basic knowledge of Physics, I thought it would be appropriate to examine the problem of *raga-rasa* in an empirical manner. The acoustical perspective adopted in the present study has led to an objective evaluation of the *raga-rasa* relation. The present volume is an edited version of the work that constituted my doctoral dissertation submitted to the S.N.D.T. University, Bombay in 1993. Although several additions to the reference material on *raga-rasa* have been made,the experimental data remains unrevised since no similar study has hence been conducted to alter radically, the interpretations presented by me. However, a comprehensive review of the experiments and concepts is definitely necessary.

I hope that the present endeavour has shown a new approach to resolve the complex issue of *raga-rasa*.

SUVARNALATA RAO

Mumbai
1 October 1999

Acknowledgements

I am deeply indebted to my respected Guruji Pandit Arvind Parikh, under whose tutelage I have the privilege to undergo music training. The insight I have gained through this training constitutes an inseparable part of this study. It was my good fortune to be constantly guided by Dr. Prabha Atre, an eminent vocalist, throughout the course of this work. This endeavour could not have been accomplished but for the sophisticated 'Melodic Movement Analyzer' designed and perfected by Dr. Bernard Bel, Centre National De La Recherche Scientifique, Marseille, France. I am grateful to Dr. Bel for his constant encouragement and guidance, personally and through correspondence throughout the period of this study. The help rendered by Dr. Wim van der Meer, who provided an opportunity to verify my results with an independent system (LVS) in the Department der Letteren, University of Leiden, The Netherlands, is gratefully acknowledged. Elaborate discussions I had with Dr. Wim van der Meer and some of his data related to this work have been incorporated into this book. I express my sincere gratitude to Dr. S.A.K. Durga, Director, Centre for Ethnomusicology, Madras, for the systematic training I received from her in research methodology and for the constructive criticism offered by her throughout the course of this work. I am also grateful to my teacher Prof. P.S. Vanjape, Department of Physics, K.C. College, Bombay, who introduced me to the world of acoustics and provided the initial impetus for undertaking this objective study. This work could not have been possible but for the laboratory facilities and the archival recordings provided by the National Centre for the Performing Arts, Bombay. The role played by Mr. D.B. Biswas, Executive Director, NCPA, Bombay, by his keen interest and personal involvement in this study deserves a special mention. The importance of the invaluable erudite discussions that I held with Dr. A.D. Ranade, the well-known musician and musicologist, on many aspects of this work, cannot be overemphasized. The help provided by a good friend Ms. Jane Harvey, World Music Department., Rotterdam Conservatory, The Netherlands, in editing some of the chapters of this monograph, is kindly acknowledged. The assistance given by Dr. Shrimathi Madiman in preparing the index is gratefully acknowledged. I owe a special debt to my dear husband Dr. B.S. Rao for his patience, love and unstinted support.

I am grateful to the University Grants Commission for granting me a research fellowship to undertake this work for the period of five years from January 1987 to December 1991.

Introduction

Raga and *rasa*, are the two prominent terms that invariably figure in the context of Indian classical music and Indian aesthetics, respectively. Association of a specific *rasa* (aesthetic emotion) with *svara* (note), *jati* (ancient modal pattern) and *dhruva* (*jati*-based vocal compositions) as theorized by Bharata, finally culminated into *raga-rasa* relation. In spite of the two long millennia that have passed after the postulation of *rasa* theory, the concept still survives in the literature on music with all its essential details. On the performing front, the *raga*-performances invariably reflect a characteristic 'aesthetic atmosphere'. Further, the ability of the performer to invoke the characteristic aesthetic atmosphere of a *raga*, is a measure of one's musicianship. Hence, the training, practice as well as the performance related to *raga* reveal the musicians' efforts being constantly directed towards creation of the aforesaid 'atmosphere', often described using colloquial expressions such as *raga-bhava, mahaul, ranga, prakriti* etc.

Nonetheless, when directly questioned, most of the performers today hardly ever show any concern towards the aspect of *rasa*. The music-*rasa* principle was enunciated in the context of Gana type of music, which constituted an integral part of drama, as it was essentially employed to highlight the mental states involved in a drama. Due to the basic differences in the *jati*-based Gana type of music and the *raga*-based contemporary music, there are serious limitations in extending the paraphernalia associated with the former to the latter. As a result, musicologists and a minority of academically oriented musicians having insight into the subject have expressed serious reservations about the direct extension of *rasa* theory to *raga*-music. Further, in the light of subjectivity involved in *raga*-performance as well as that related to the performers and listeners; changed socio-cultural values and the aesthetic norms, the specificity attached to *raga-rasa* relation has become a questionable issue. Hence, the musicians seem to be hesitant in accepting the idea of associating a *raga* with a specific *rasa*. This discussion might suggest that the formulations regarding the *raga-rasa* theory have perhaps reduced to no more than mere theoretical formulae bearing no practical significance at the level of performance. Thus, there appears to be a gap between the textual tradition of *raga*-music and the performing tradition of *raga*-music, regarding the attribution of a particular *rasa* to a *raga*.

The present endeavour is aimed at abridging the divergence that exists between the theory of *rasa* and its actual realization in the context of contemporary *raga*-music. Although a consistent relation between a *raga* and a specific *rasa* cannot be logically defended, the fact that a *raga* projects a characteristic musical idea resulting into a unique aesthetic atmosphere capable of arousing a neuro-psychological response, cannot be ruled out. As often experienced by the performers and the connoisseurs of Indian classical music,the highest level of aesthetic experience akin to *Brahmananda* or the eternal bliss is a reality in music. The present work is based on this premise.

A scientific approach to further our understanding of 'aesthetic appeal' resulting from a *raga*-performance ought to include a physical analysis at the level of the source as well the physiological and psychological studies at the level of perception. The present study however, restricts itself to only the physical (acoustical) investigation of the source of music.

The 'tonal configuration' related to a *raga* is the most significant aspect that has been traditionally accepted to influence the 'aesthetic appeal' or the *rasa* at the perceptible level. Since aspects of 'intonation' and 'melodic movement' together constitute the 'tonal configuration', these aspects have been analyzed. Considering the problems of correlating the physically measured parameter of 'frequency' representing the pitch (intonation), audibly perceived parameter of 'tonal configuration' and visually evaluated element of 'melodic shapes' (through melodic contours obtained on the computer monitor) with the neuro-psychologically perceived abstract feelings, the scope of this study is limited to ascertain the presence of similar intonation and melodic movements in the performance of a given *raga* by different performers.

Such similitude, if found, can suggest a correlation between the tonal configuration of a *raga* and its aesthetic effect. Analysis of *alapa* in a performance of *khayal* in *raga Yaman* rendered by the late Ustad Amir Khan, Pandit Bhimsen Joshi and Dr. Prabha Atre has been carried out using two independent computer set-ups, viz. 'Melodic Movement Analyzer' (MMA) and 'LVS'.

Although the above systems can objectively evaluate pitch its interpretation for aesthetic relevance demands a constant involvement of a musically trained person, which brings in subjectivity into the study. Considering a fresh approach required for the present study, a working methodology had to be evolved by trial and error method after getting acquainted with the routine procedures involved in operating the system in various modes. A pilot study was conducted to test the validity of this methodology. These preliminary procedures aimed at standardizing the technique for analysis of intonation and melodic movement of a *raga* performed in the north Indian classical tradition (henceforth simply referred to as Indian music) were found to be laborious and time-consuming.

The *rasa*-theory formulated by Bharata and its application to *svara* (notes), *jatis* (modal patterns) and *dhruvas* (songs) was exclusively in the context of drama, which include the art of music. In the later period many *lakshana-granthas* (authoritative treatises on the grammatical aspects) on music have upheld the same associations in the form of *raga-rasa*. Even when music was recognized as an art independent of the drama, equations relating a *raga* and a specific *rasa* continued to flourish. In the absence of visual (histrionics) and/or textual element (as in the case of instrumental music, the traditional paraphernalia of cause-effect (*vibhava-anubhava*) associated with the *rasa* theory, can be applied only to the tonal structure. This limitation has been already recognized by the contemporary musicologists like Dr. Premlata Sharma, Acharya Brihaspati, Thakur Jaideva Singh and others. Having realized the truth about the eternal bliss resulting from music, they have suggested new approaches of theoretical nature for restating the *rasa* theory in the context of contemporary *raga*-music.

In the present study, an empirical approach has been adopted for examining the *raga-rasa* theory. The similitude of tonal configuration comprising intonation and melodic movement observed in the performance of a *raga* by different vocalists, allows to correlate tonal configuration of the *raga* with its unique identity and consequently with the aesthetic atmosphere projected through that *raga*. The findings of this study prove that a *raga* has a characteristic atmosphere. The elements such as the *sahitya* (text) and *laya* (tempo), together with the variant factors like the tonal quality of voice and instrument, do bring in various shades of moods which are of transitory nature. The traditionally prescribed *rasas* like *Shringara, Karuna, Shanta* etc. may be perceived at times in this context. The present endeavour suggests that the aesthetic effect due to the tonal configuration of a *raga*, constitutes a core of the total experience or the *rasa*, while the effect due to the varying elements constitutes its periphery. The wholesome combination of the two aforesaid factors lead to an integrated effect of *rasa*. However, absolutely no specificity can be attached to this experience in terms of a specific *rasa*. It can be described as *gana-rasa* or the *rasa* emerging from a musical exposition. Whatever be the nature of transitory moods, the *gana-rasa* leads one to an experience which is said to be akin to the *Brahmananda* or the bliss experienced upon the knowledge of the ultimate reality.

CHAPTER 1

The Emergence of the Raga-Rasa Concept

The concept of *rasa*

The Hindu perception of art and literature may be said to rely mainly on the aesthetic conception of *rasa*. It is the most important term that emerged in the formal theory of enjoyment of art and literature in India from very early times. The use of the term *rasa* in the context of arts in India is widespread, and it forms a central part of performing arts vocabulary as well as in related literature.

Interpretations of the term *rasa*

The Sanskrit word *rasa* is derived from the root *ras*, meaning 'to taste'. It is one of those Sanskrit words whose precise significance is as diverse as its usage. Before being introduced into the realm of art, the term *rasa* was used in literature, the Vedas and Upanishads. The sense in which it figures in the sacred Hindu literature and that used in the context of art, widely differ. The term *rasa* occurs in the *Rigveda* to mean the juice of the *soma* plant, i.e. *soma-rasa* (1X.63.13; 65.15). In the earlier hymns, it signifies milk or water and sometimes denotes flavour (V.44.13; VIII.72.13). In addition to its earlier meaning as the juice of plants and herbs, in the *Atharvaveda* (III.31.10) it is used to denote the sap of grain. During the Upanishadic times, in par with other Vedic concepts that developed from the particular to the universal, the term *rasa* assumed an abstract connotation of 'essential element' or 'essence', abandoning different connotations such as water, milk, sap of grain, etc. (*Brh. Up.*, I.3.19). However, it is in the *Taittiriya Upanishad* that the term *rasa* seems to have acquired a philosophical significance (*Taittiriya Up.*, II.7). In these scriptures, *rasa* denotes the 'ultimate reality' which is the basis of *ananda* or the highest state of bliss. As noted by many scholars,the concept of *rasa* in the parlance of art cannot be positively defined because it is supposed to be intuitively realised rather than sensibly experienced.

The different connotations of *rasa* could be viewed as having significance on three different levels—the physical, the psychological and the metaphysical. In the physical sense, it is used to denote juice or essence. For instance, when one states that the fruit is full of *rasa*, it means that it is full of juice. In the psychological sense, it implies flavour or taste where the active participation of psyche plays a definite role, while on the metaphysical level it describes the experience that one undergoes when aroused by an artistic expression. The perceiver enjoys an experience which is exalted from the particular to the universal plane by bringing about a complete effacement of the experiencer's ego and its total identification with that artistic creation. It is this supra-mundane experience described in the Upanishads that assumes significance in Indian aesthetics.

Aesthetic relevance

The credit for adopting the concept of *rasa*, hitherto confined to Vedic literature, in the realm of the performing arts, has been given to Bharata (300 BC-AD 200), whose monumental treatise *Natyashastra* is the first available work on dramaturgy. Attributing the authorship of the science of drama to Brahma (the divine creator), Bharata states that Brahma created *Natya* or the fifth Veda by absorbing different elements from the existing four Vedas. Brahma adopted *pathya* (verbal text) from *Rigveda*, *gita* (music) from *Samaveda*, *abhinaya* (histrionic expression) from *Yajurveda* and *rasa* from *Atharvaveda* (*Natyashastra*, 1.7). Recognising *rasa* as the goal of all artistic activities, he states that the major function of different art-forms is only to evoke *rasa* in a percipient. Further he elaborates that in a literary work or play there should be no place for wasteful words, sentences or emotions which do not contribute to the creation of *rasa*. A performance of dance or music might often be criticized as being devoid of *rasa (nirasa)* or praised for yielding *rasa* in great measure. The order in which Bharata has enumerated the eleven essential aspects of drama is very significant, in that he has placed *rasa* before all the other elements. The extraordinary bliss of *rasa* that one enjoys by virtue of a work of art like poetry, music or drama, has been elaborately described and discussed, first by Bharata and later by many scholars. Although the *rasa* theory had been initially propounded as an essential element of *natya* (dramatic art), it was later on applied to *kavya* (poetry) and other fine arts such as *alekhya* (drawing and painting), *sangita* (music), *nritya* (histrionic expressions of dance), *murtishilpa* (sculpture) and *vastushilpa* or architecture.

Categories of *rasas*

Bharata has classified *rasa* into eight categories (*Natyashastra*, VI). The idea of eight different forms of *rasa* does not imply that *rasa* is either qualitatively or quantitatively divisible into eight species but rather suggests that these eight are "the various colourings of one experience". Thus the word *rasa* may be employed relatively, in plural with respect to various conditions which constitute the burden of a given work. These are *Shringara* (amorous), *Hasya* (humorous), *Karuna* (pathetic), *Raudra* (furious), *Vira* (valorous), *Bhayanaka* (horrific), *Bibhatsa* (repugnant), and *Adbhuta* or wondrous. Bharata also states eight *sthayi bhavas* or static emotions, eight *sattvika bhavas* or responsive emotions and thirty-three *sanchari/vyabhichari bhavas* or the transitory emotions. The eight static emotions that are responsible for the eight *rasas*, in order, are: *rati* (love), *hasa* (mirth), *shoka* (grief), *krodha* (anger), *utsaha* (enthusiasm), *bhaya* (fear), *jugupsa* (disgust) and *vismaya* (surprise). The eight static emotions in conjunction with their associated group of *sanchari* and *sattvika bhavas*, may evoke corresponding *rasas*. Apart from the eight *rasas* proposed by Bharata, several later authors on this subject have suggested other *rasas*. These include *Preyas* or *Vatsalya* (affection) and *Bhakti* (devotion) by Udbhata, *Shanta* (calm) by Abhinavagupta, *Brahma* by Haripala, etc. Although, yet some other forms of *rasas* such as *Vyasana, Dukkha, Udatta, Madhura, Karpanya,* etc. have also been suggested, only the *Shanta rasa* suggested by Abhinavagupta has been widely accepted along with the eight *rasas* proposed by Bharata.

Subdivisions and interdependence of *rasas*

The exhaustive deliberation on the subject of *rasa* by Bharata includes several subdivisions of each *rasa*.

Bharata states that there are only four main independent *rasas*, and the remaining four *rasas* are dependent on them. The independent *rasas* are *Shringara* (amorous), *Vira* (valorous), *Raudra* (furious), and *Bibhatsa* (repugnant). The *Hasya rasa* (humorous) is dependent on *Shringara* (amorous), *Karuna* (pathetic) on *Raudra* (furious), *Adbhuta* (wondrous) on *Vira* (valorous) and *Bhayanaka* (horrific) on *Bibhatsa* or repugnant (*Natyashastra,* VI.39-41).

The *raga* concept in Indian music

Raga, as understood in contemporary musical parlance, eludes a simple and concise definition. In a broader sense it could be termed as a melodic mode or a matrix possessing rigid and specific individuality, yet bearing an immense potential for infinite improvisatory melodic possibilities. Today *raga* is the predominant concept in Indian art music, so much so that the two have become almost synonymous. Practically every aspect of Indian art music seems to pertain to *raga*. The documented evidence available today is very scanty with regards to tracing the processes by which *ragas* have evolved to their present forms and characters.

Rasas	*No. of subdivisions*	*Name assigned/types*
Shringara (amorous)	2	*samyoga* (union) *viyoga* (separation)
Hasya (humorous)	6	*smita* (gentle smile) *hasita* (smile) *vihasita* (laughter) *upahasita* (laughter with ridicule) *apahasita* (uproarious laughter) *atihasita* (convulsive laughter)
Karuna (pathetic)	3	sorrow destruction of order reduction of wealth
Raudra (furious)	3	action costume speech
Vira (valorous)	3	*daanavira* (valour in giving away) *dharmavira* (valour in following righteous path) *yuddhavira* (valour in fight)
Bhayanaka (horrific)	3	fictitious horror horror due to a grievous mistake horror due to fear-complex
Bibhatsa (repugnant)	2	excitement created by seeing disgusting insects, etc., infliction created by looking at blood, intestines, etc.
Adbhuta (wondrous)	2	exquisite, pleasurable

However, a survey of the surviving authoritative treatises on this subject can help to throw some light on the evolution of the *raga*-concept.

The nucleus of *raga*-concept can be seen in the *Natyashastra* attributed to the sage Bharata. Out of the three *gramas* (basic parent scales) that existed in ancient times, the *Gandhara grama* was obsolete by Bharata's period. Thus the 18 *jatis* (modal patterns) discussed by Bharata are formulated according to the two remaining *gramas*, viz. the *Shadja grama* and *Madhyama grama*, as shown in Table 1.

TABLE 1
Jatis enumerated by Bharata

Jatis of Shadja grama	*Jatis of Madhyama grama*
Shadji	*Gandhari*
Arshabhi	*Madhyama*
Dhaivati	*Panchami*
Naishadi	*Gandharodichyava*
Shadjodichyavati	*Gandhara-panchami*
Shadja-kaishiki	*Rakta-gandhari*
Shadja-madhyama	*Madhyamodichyava*
	Nandayanti
	Karmaravi
	Andhri
	Kaishiki

(*Natyashastra,* XXVIII.41-45

These *jatis* (7 of *Shadja grama* and 11 of *Madhyama grama* were derived from *gramas* by applying the principle c *murchhana* which essentially involves a shift of tonic, leadin to different arrangements of the seven notes in a give *grama.* Each of these *jatis* was supposed to have two varieties– *Shuddha* or pure and *Vikrita* or deplete. *Shadji, Arshabh Dhaivati,* and *Naishadi* of *Shadja grama* and *Gandhari, Mad yama* and *Panchami* of *Madhyama grama* are reckoned as pur melodies and the rest are considered to be deplete or *Vikri* varieties of melodies.

Bharata prescribes ten *lakshanas* or the characteristics th governern *jatis.* They are *graha* (initial note), *amsa* (fundament or dominant note), *nyasa* (final note), *apanyasa* (semi-fin note), *tara* (highest limit of the tonal range), *mandra* (lowe limit of the tonal range), *alpatva* (sparcity of notes), *bahut* (abundance of notes), *sadava* (hexatonic structure) an *audava* (pentatonic structure). These *lakshanas* were th guidelines for creating the melodic matrix of *jati* from th parent scale or *grama.*

In addition to elaborations on *jatis,* Bharata's text al refers to seven musical entities called *grama ragas.* They a *Shadva, Madhyama grama, Shadja grama, Sadharita, Pancham*

Kaishika and *Kaishika-madhyama.* These *grama-ragas* were employed at particular junctures (*sandhis*) of a drama.

The next authoritative treatise which we can refer to after Bharata's time, is the *Brihaddeshi* of Matanga (AD 500-800). Apart from a chapter containing discussion on *jatis*, *Brihaddeshi* provides a special chapter on *ragas.* This treatise is considered to be an important landmark in the history of *ragas,* since it is here that the expression *raga* was used and defined for the first time in the sense it is understood to date. Although Bharata does not use the expression *raga* as defined by Matanga and his followers, Bharata's *jatis* (and *jati-lakshanas*) provide the genus out of which *ragas* have evolved. Matanga defines *raga* as:

> *"Svara-varna-visesana dhvani-bhedena va punah.*
> *Rajyate yena yah kaschit sa ragah sammatah satam."*
>
> (*Brihaddeshi,* v. 263)

It means, "That which colours the mind of the good through a specific *svara* (interval) and *varna* (melodic movement) or through a type of *dhvani* (sound) is known by the wise as *raga.*[1]

Matanga regards *raga* as one of the seven classes of songs current in his time. These melodies are known under the generic name of *gitis,* one of which represented the *raga-gitis* or the 'melodies proper'.

The eight varieties of *raga-gitis* were further divided to obtain a number of *ragas.*

Unfortunately the successive developments in the evolutionary process of *raga* are not supported by documents, as there is a considerable gap between Matanga and the next landmark, i.e. the *Sangita Makaranda* of Narada (AD 700-900). It is in this treatise that the *ragas* have been classified into masculine melodies *(pumlinga-raga),* feminine melodies *(stri-raga)* and neuter melodies (*napumsaka-raga*). The principle of classification is according to the *rasa* evoked by the particular melody. It is also the earliest text to have proposed the association of particular seasons and hours of the day with each *raga.*[2]

TABLE 2(A)
Classification of *gitis*

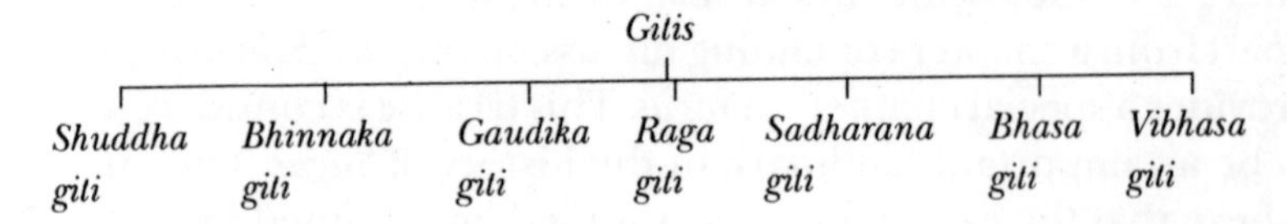

Of these seven classes of *gitis*, subdivisions are also enumerated by the author.

TABLE 2(B)
Subdivisions of *gitis*

Gitis	*Number of sub-divisions or varieties*
Shuddha	Five
Bhinnaka	Five
Gaudika	Three
Raga	Eight
Sadharana	Six
Bhasa	Sixteen
Vibhasa	Twelve

The next important step in the advancement of the *raga*-concept is documented in the *Bharata-bhashya* (also known as *Saraswati-hridayalankara*) ascribed to king Nanyabhupala (alias Nanyadeva, AD 1097-1133). Two chapters (the sixth and seventh) of this text are devoted to describe the *lakshana* (structure), *rupaka* (notation) and *alapaka* (improvisatory aspect) of *raga* presentation. This aspect of *alapaka* is very significant in the sense that it contributed an added dimension to the existing form of *raga*-delineation. The text also bears information regarding the presiding deity and specific season for each *raga*. Besides, this text also describes seven different types of *gamakas* (embellishments) employed by musicians to ornament the tonal structures.[3]

The *Sangita Ratnakara* of Sharngadeva (AD 1247) is regarded as one of the major works ever produced in the field of Indian music. It provides immense information on various subjects such as *gayan* (vocal music), *tala* (rhythm), *vadya* (instruments), *nritya* (histrionic expressions of dance) and *rasa*. After having provided the details of *raga-lakshanas* (which are similar to *jati-lakshanas*), the author describes *raga*-elaboration. The process is explained under three expressions, viz., *upohana, alapa,* and *alapti*. *Upohana* included melodic phrases to be sung prior to the rendering of *dhruva* songs. These phrases used meaningless syllables and were designed around the *sthayi* note. Besides projecting the character of the *raga,* this process also helped to indicate *tala* (rhythm) of the song which followed. As defined by Simhabhupala, melodic phrases stressing the contrasting notes (*tirobhava*) constituted *alapti,* whereas emphasis on the *sthayi* note of the *raga* (*avirbhava*) was known as *alapa*. These means of *raga*-exposition were independent of *prabandha* songs and *tala* (rhythm). Further, this text provides a detailed account of so-called *adhuna-prasiddha* or currently popular *ragas* with their *raga-alapa* or the melodic elaborations. *Sangita Ratnakara* happens to be the first musical text to provide explicit data regarding the *rasa* aspect of *desi-ragas** along with valuable information on the occasion and time for their rendering (II.77-89). The idea of using aids such as *tirobhava* (contrasting notes), various *gamakas* (embellishment) and *kaku* (tonal and other type of inflections) in addition to the existing *raga-lakshanas* for portraying the proper identity of a *raga,* seems to have gained importance during the time of Sharngadeva.[4]

Contemporary to *Sangita Ratnakara* of Sharngadeva, there is yet another important treatise, viz. Parshvadeva's *Sangita Samayasara* (1250). It presents a novel way of classifying the existing *ragas* into divisions of *raganga, bhashanga, upanga* and *kriyanga*.[5] Besides delineating rules regarding the performance of many *ragas* (*raga-chalan*), it provides valuable information on sixteen types of *alaptis* (the various methods for *raga*-elaboration) along with the seven types of *gamakas*. (I.26-41 and 47-55).

*The *ragas* which did not conform to the rigorous structure of *grama* and were born out of deviations from the same, were called *desi-ragas*. The system of *dhyana* (visual contemplation) seems to have originated in their context.

The expressions *alapti, alapaka, upohana* etc. that have been mentioned so far by various authors are of special significance, since in the present work *alapa* (which has a similar connotation and function to these expressions in the present day Indian-music) has been analysed to understand the tonal structure of a *raga.*

The *raga*-concept had completely developed by this time and hence many authors after this date have quoted details of *raga*-structure, their number and nomenclature etc. as expounded by Sharngadeva in *Sangita Ratnakara.*

By the twelfth century, differentiation in the classification of *ragas* marked a break between the Northern and Southern systems. While the Southern system remained more or less immune to external influences, the Northern system seems to have undergone significant changes around the fourteenth century. Under royal patronage, Muslim and Persian musicians such as Amir Khusro judiciously combined Persian melodies with Indian *ragas* and introduced many derivative melodies hitherto unknown to the Indian system.

Treatises written during the fifteenth century reveal the influence of the Hindu doctrine of 'image-worship' upon music, e.g. Narada's *Pancham Sarasamhita* cites contemplative verses or *dhyana* and iconographic pictures for *ragas,* thus adding a new thought to supplement the *raga*-concept.[6] The same idea is evident in the *Sangita Damodara* of Shubhankara, who describes *raga-lakshanas* (rules for *ragas*) in the form of *kavyamaya dhyanas* (contemplative poetic verses). These associations suggest that a *raga* was believed to have a psychic form which could be visualised through the poetic verses. The deity that is supposed to be presiding over the *raga,* could be invoked by *dhyana* or the prayer.

The details of *gamakas* (some of them are practised even to this day) are mentioned by Somanath in his treatise, *Raga-vibodha* (AD 1610) along with information on their articulation (5, 14-22). In Venkatmakhi's *Chaturdandi-prakashika* (AD 1620), the author explains different stages of *alapa,* indicating its increasing importance in *raga* performance. (6, 1-32)

The writings of the eighteenth and nineteenth centuries do not provide additional information on the *raga*-concept but indicate the addition of new *ragas* and novel methods for their classification. From the nucleus of *jati* that emerged from *grama* (the parent scale) in Bharata's time, a revolutionary musical thought of *raga* was introduced by Matanga. The concept developed with respect to structure, exposition etc. and assumed a concrete shape by the time of Sharngadeva. During the later period, although immense modifications occurred, the core of the *raga*-concept seems to have remained unchanged. Each *raga* was linked with many extra-musical elements such as specific colour, deity, time and season for their singing, *dhyana, rasa* etc. *Raga* being a sonal body of abstract nature, these extra-generic references might have been attached to personify it in a concrete form.

References

1. Premlata Sharma, ed., p. 77.
2. *Sangita Makaranda,* p. 15.
3. *Bharata-bhashya,* ch. V, vv. 18-23.
4. Vide Gamaka-prakarana in ch. II.
5. *Sangita Samayasara,* p. 15.
6. Ch. III, vv. 26-67.

CHAPTER 2

Raga-Rasa as Expounded in Ancient, Medieval and Modern Works

Music as a product of human skill and artistic endeavour, embodies selectively organized sounds and rhythm interspersed with silence. This can arouse psycho-physiological responses transcending cultural barriers. However, specific extra-musical associations such as music-emotion or music-colour may be influenced by ethnocultural factors.

The spiritual basis accorded to music in ancient Indian culture is evident from the practice of attaching extra-musical references and associations to various musical entities. Some such associations have resulted from the influence of Vedantic and Tantric philosophy. For instance; in Vedic tradition, every hymn or *sukta* is endowed with a seer, presiding deity, and so on. The association of specific deity, colour, gender, visual contemplation (*dhyana*), time of the day, season and *rasa* with a particular *svara, jati, raga* etc. are nothing but attempts to personify abstract musical entities. Outwardly, such references may appear to be mystical but they do succeed in creating projections of musical entities (particularly *raga*) as having separate identities. These are not mere products of fanciful imagination but are well-meaning attempts to bring a holistic approach to the art of music. However, modern attitudes of agnosticism and atheism have led to the non-existence of such a philosophic outlook.

The Hindu philosophy firmly believed in interrelationship of various arts in general and that of graphic art and the art of music in particular. An anecdote from the ancient *Shilpa-*

shastra elucidates the interdependence of arts like image-making, painting, dancing, instrumental music and vocal music; and asserts that music is the source and end of all the other arts.

Bharata expounded the *rasa* theory for the art of stage, i.e. *natya*, which incorporated dance and music. His deliberations on *rasa* indicate that all the elements of *natya* like music, dance, dress, make-up etc. should be directed to achieve the desired *rasa*. The detailed discussion offered by Bharata in this connection has provided basic guidelines for the application of *rasa* theory to other arts like music, dance, poetry (all independent of dramatic art), painting and sculpture. In fact, it has been surmised that in later times, extrageneric associations such as *raga-dhyana* were linked to music so as to fill the void caused by separating music from the context of drama.[1]

From Bharata up to now, numerable theories have been proposed by several musicologists regarding the various musical entities such as *svara, jati, raga,* etc., and their *rasa*. Each of these theories will be discussed alongwith their essential characteristics. For the sake of clarity and convenience, these are listed in three sections, viz., the ancient Sanskrit works (from Bharata to eleventh century), works of the medieval period (from Sharngadeva to nineteenth century), and modern works in English as well as in other regional languages, written from the nineteenth century to this time.

Raga-rasa as expounded in the ancient Sanskrit works

Bharata's Natyashastra

Although the great sage-poet Valmiki describes in *Ramayana* (400 BC) the aesthetic sentiment of seven *shuddha jati-ragas* like *Shadji, Arshabhi, Gandhari,* etc., Bharata's *Natyashastra* seems to be one of the first treatises on drama that deals with music and *rasa* in great depth. Nearly eight chapters from 28 to 34 are devoted to discussions on music.

Though the subject of music is auxiliary, the comprehensive nature of the discussions has made it an authoritative text on music.

After having expounded the *rasa* theory in the context of drama, Bharata proceeds to explain its application to various entities of music as well. As noted earlier, drama as it was understood in Bharata's time incorporated dance and music in the art of the stage. Music as defined by Bharata included songs, instrumental music and dance. As a consequence, enjoining different musical entities (as they were used in drama) with different *rasas* was quite justified. The relation between a specific *svara* (note), *jati* (ancient modal pattern) and *dhruva* (*jati*-based vocal composition) with a particular *rasa*, has been clearly mentioned by Bharata.

Bharata's *Natyashastra* provides evidence to believe that two separate categories of music were in vogue during that time. The category of music that stood independent of a dramatic situation was called Gandharva, whereas, that which was employed to highlight the mental states involved in a given situation of drama was known as Gana. The connection between music and *rasa* as discussed by Bharata, pertains exclusively to the latter category of music i.e., Gana. Bharata also refers to the use of particular musical entities such as certain *grama-ragas*, to be employed at a definite juncture or *sandhi* of the drama, rather than to promote particular mental states.

The *rasas* associated with different *svaras* as enumerated by Bharata are as follows:

TABLE 3
Association of *rasa* and *svara*

Svaras	*Rasas*
Madhyama, Panchama	*Shringara, Hasya*
Shadja, Rishabha	*Vira, Raudra, Adbhuta,*
Gandhara, Nishada	*Karuna*
Dhaivata	*Bibhatsa, Bhayanaka*

However, these associations do not assume using these *svaras* in isolation. Bharata's own delineation in this regard (ibid., 29.12-15) suggests that these *svaras* have to be made *amsha svara* (principal notes). However, quoting the same verses of Bharata, Shringy interprets these *svaras* as referring to the tonic or the first note of the *murchhana*. Hence the *rasa* associated with a particular tone is not produced by the tone in isolation but by the *murchhana* commenced on that tone.[2]

In the context of *jatis* (ancient modal patterns), Bharata enumerates their corresponding *rasas* in the following order:

TABLE 4
Association of *rasa* and *jatis*

Rasas	*Jatis to be employed*
Shringara	*Shadja-madhyama, Madhyama, Panchami, Shadjodichyavati* and *Nandayanti*
Hasya	Ibid.
Karuna	*Shadja-kaishiki, Gandhari, Rakta-gandhari* and *Shadja-madhyama*
Raudra	*Shadji, Arshabhi, Madhyamodichyava, Gandharadichyava* and *Shadja-madhyama*
Vira	Ibid.
Bhayanaka	*Dhaivati, Kaishiki, Gandhara-panchami* and *Shadja-madhyama*
Bibhatsa	Ibid.
Adbhuta	*Shadji, Arshabhi, Andhri, Karmaravi* and *Shadja-madhyama*

(*Natyashastra,* XXIX.1-14)

In addition to his exposition concerning the relationship between *svaras* and *jatis* with a specific *rasa,* Bharata has also discussed *rasa* theory in the context of *dhruvas* or the *jati*-based vocal compositions (*Natyashastra,* XXXII.371-83), e.g. *Apakrishta dhruva* should be sung in a pathetic sentiment; or in physical distress and in anger, *Antara dhruva* should be employed. (ibid.)

The relationship of various *svaras, jatis* and *dhruvas* with specific *rasas* as expounded by Bharata cannot be accepted in the context of present-day music. Firstly because the connection between music and *rasa* as discussed by Bharata pertains to the Gana type of music which was integrated in *natya* or the drama proper. Secondly, the *jati*-based music has become *raga*-based and finally, the art of music is no more an element of drama.

Matanga's Brihaddeshi

Quoting the passage of Bharata, Matanga in his treatise *Brihaddeshi* (AD 500-800), mentions that the *Madhyama grama* melodies should be used in the *mukha* (opening of the drama), the *Shadja grama* melodies in the *pratimukha* stages (progression), the *Sadharita* melodies in the *garbha* (development) stages, and the *Panchama jati* melodies for the *vimarsha* (pause) and so on.[3] Further, in describing the component notes of each *giti* or the *jati* type of melody, Matanga mentions the *rasa* or the flavour of sentiment appropriate to each along with its place in the body of drama. It is surmised that the *raga-gitis* were first distinguished from other classes of *gitis* like *Shuddha, Bhinna, Gaudi,* etc. on account of *rasa* or the power of evoking a clearly differentiated sentiment.[4]

Narada's Sangita Makaranda

In *Sangita Makaranda* (AD 700-900) attributed to Narada, melodies are classified into masculine melodies (*pumlinga-raga*), feminine melodies (*strilinga-raga*) and neuter melodies (*napumsaka-raga*). This classification is based on the character of *rasa* evoked by the *raga*. Narada elaborates that the masculine melodies are to be employed for creating feelings of passion, admiration or heroism; for sentiments like love, humour and sorrow, feminine melodies should be employed; while the neuter melodies are used to evoke terror, abhorrence and peace.[5] The major melodies and their corresponding emotive values, as cited by Matanga, do not figure in the list of Narada. Hence, a comparison relating the *rasa* attributed to the melodies prevailing during the respective periods cannot be attempted.

Raga-rasa as expounded in the medieval treatises

Sharngadeva's Sangita Ratnakara

In the monumental work known as *Sangita Ratnakara* (AD 1247), Sharngadeva quotes Bharata for providing a relationship between each *svara* and its specific *rasa.* He presents an exhaustive survey of *jatis, grama-ragas* and *desi-ragas.* Then in describing the *adhuna-prasiddha ragas,* Sharngadeva enumerates the *rasa* of some of the *grama-ragas* (*ragas* strictly associated with drama) and *desi-ragas* (*ragas* which were out of the fold of the *grama*-structure). Thus *raga Bhinna-shadja* and *raga Bhairava* have been associated with *Bibhatsa* and *Bhayanaka rasa, ragas Todi* and *Bengal* are associated with *Harsha* while *Gurjari raga* is linked with *Shringara rasa.* In the chapter entitled 'Raga-viveka,' detailed information is available regarding nearly sixty *ragas* and their *rasa* (see Appendix 1).

However, the specific information relating to *raga* and *rasa* presented in this work can have practically no relevance to present-day *raga*-music. In spite of the detailed descriptions of various *ragas* presented by Sharngadeva, we have no real evidence to link the *ragas* of today with those discussed in this work, even though some of the *ragas* bear the same names.

Commentary by Simhabhupala and Kallinatha on Sangita Ratnakara

Simhabhupala's critical work (AD 1385) on Sharngadeva's *Sangita Ratnakara* proposes that the nomenclature assigned to *sruti-jatis* by Bharata is indicative of the emotive power of the respective *shruti.*[6] Kallinatha (AD 1450), the other commentator of *Sangita Ratnakara* seems to agree with this view. Incidentally, the same idea has been later upheld by Ahobala in *Sangita Parijata.*

Shardatanaya's Bhavaprakashan

Even though five and half chapters of the work entitled *Bhavaprakashan* (AD 1250) authored by Shardatanaya are devoted to discussions on *rasa* and *bhava,* the text of these chapters mainly contains surveys of the views expressed by his predecessors, including Bharata, Narada, Abhinavagupta, Rudrata, Sharngadeva and so on. Hence, practically no original information is offered regarding *raga-rasa* by this author.

Rana Kumbha's Sangitaraja

The unique contribution of this work is the view that each *raga* has its appropriate time measure (*tala*) which brings out the genius of the *raga* in its characteristic qualities. The author seems to suggest that it is the time-measure which reveals its real flavour. Although it does not imply that a *raga* can only be interpreted in a fixed time-measure, it does suggests that particular *ragas* can best be interpreted and expressed in particular time-measures.

Srikantha's Rasakaumudi

The *Rasakaumudi* of Srikantha (AD1575) offers descriptions of many *melas* and *janya-ragas* (II.79-169). However, only a few *raga* are discussed with respect to their *rasa*. Comparing the specific *rasa* assigned in *Sangita Ratnakara* with that suggested in *Rasakaumudi* in the case of a few *ragas*, we observe that the *rasas* suggested for a particular *raga* by these two authors are not very different. Of course, here we presume that the following *ragas* have not changed significantly in their tonal structure and hence melodies with the same names are taken to represent identical *ragas*.

TABLE 5
Comparison of *rasas* attributed by Sharngadeva and Srikantha

Ragas	*Rasas according to Sangita Ratnakara*	*Rasas according to Rasakaumudi*
Panchama	*Shringara, Hasya*	*Shringara*
Dhannasi	*Vira*	*Vira*
Todi	*Harsha*	pleases mind
Velavali	*Vipralambha*	*Vira*

Kitab-i-Nauras of Ibrahim Adilshah II (Persian)

The above work embodies a collection of songs composed by Ibrahim Adilshah II (AD 1580-1627). These songs were intended to be sung in the melodies of Hindustani music. It is clear that the author had in mind nine *rasas* of Indian aesthetics and wished to introduce them among Persian-speaking Muslims not conversant with the Sanskrit language.[7]

Ahobala's Sangita Parijata

In his authoritative treatise *Sangita Parijata* (AD 1650), Ahobala assigns specific *rasas* to the *shruti-jatis.*

TABLE 6
Association of *shruti-jati* and *rasa*

Shruti-jatis	*Rasas*
dipta	*Vira, Adbhuta, Raudra*
ayata	*Hasya*
mridu	*Shringara*
madhya	*Bibhatsa, Bhayanaka, Hasya, Shringara*
karuna	*Karuna*

Further, Ahobala proposes that the *rasa* of a particular *raga* depends upon the *shruti-jati* of its *amsha, graha* and *nyasa,* (vv. 493-95). *Rasas* attributed to different *svaras* (notes) by Ahobala are different from those found in *Natyashastra.* According to Ahobala,

Gandhara, Shadja	—	*Hasya*	*Nishada*	—	*Karuna*
Rishabha, Madhyama	—	*Shringara*	*Panchama*	—	*Bhayanaka*
Dhaivata	—	*Bibhatsa*			(v. 94)

In the context of contemporary *raga* performance a lot of empirical research has to be done before we can hope to have an unambiguous definition of *shruti* and *shruti-jati.* Hence, until such times, the above theory of enjoining various emotional states to the *shruti-jatis* will remain irrelevant in the present context. Furthermore, in the context of the present-day *raga*-performance, although the concepts of *graha, amsha* and *nyasa* etc. might not have changed so much, the particulars relating to them have definitely undergone a lot of changes.

Sanskrit treatises written after the fifteenth-sixteenth centuries do not provide direct information on the *raga-rasa* relationship. This may be due to the advent of a tradition of providing a *dhyana*-formula (a contemplative verse) to describe the *raga-rupa.* The *Panchamasarasamhita* of Narada (AD 1778) and *Sangita Damodara* of Shubhankara (fifteenth century) provide enormous information about prevalent *ragas* in the form of *dhyana* and iconographic pictures.[8] Treatises such as *Chatvarimsatchata Raganirupanam* (eighteenth century, attributed to Narada) provide descriptive verses indicative of the *rasa.* Verses describing the main *ragas* suggest *Vira* and *Raudra rasas.* Verses portraying the *ragini* are suggestive of *Shringara rasa* and those depicting the *putra* and *snusha* melodies (derivatives) are indicative of the delicate *Shringara rasa,* e.g. *Bhairava raga* is depicted as a sage carrying a *trishula* while his spouse *Bhairavi ragini* is described as a beautiful delicate woman.[9]

Raghunath Rath's Natyamanorama (Hindi)

Natyamanorama (AD 1702), a treatise on dance and music authored by Raghunath Rath, devotes ten verses (ch. II, vv. 69-78) to enumerate the time for singing six *ragas* and thirty-six *raginis.* The particular time assigned to each of these melodies evidently depends upon the emotive value or the *rasa* of that melody.

Another text called *Sangitamala* (AD 1750) by an anonymous author offers descriptive verses followed by Hindi notes specifying the *rasa* of each melody.[10]

The perusal of works such as the vernacular version of *Sangita Darpana* by Harivallabha (AD 1653), Deokavi's *Raga Ratnakara* (AD 1689), *Raga Kutuhala* by Kavi Radhakrishna (AD 1781),[11] *Sangitasara* by Pratap Singh Deo of Jaipur (AD 1779-1804), *Raga Kalpadruma* (AD 1843), S.M. Tagore's *Sangitasarasamgraha,* etc. reveal that these works written around and after the sixteenth century show a preference towards *raga-dhyana* and *Ragamala* pictures to describe *ragas.*

The contents of these verses and paintings, each based on the personification or deification of a musical mode, were pregnant from their beginnings with iconographic raw materials of various origins. The most obvious are the *rasa* and the performance time of the *ragas.* As compared to the brief and miniature forms of the Sanskrit prototypes, the original musical images are much amplified and elaborated in the Hindi descriptive texts. This suggests that perhaps the vernacular sources preferred more elaborate means of pictorial illustrations and musical iconography to illustrate the emotive character of a melody. Even today, though *Ragamala* paintings do not really seem to portray significant musical features, the very fact that pictorial and anthropomorphic representations became quite prominent over the 'syntactic models' in describing the individuality of each *raga,* points to important changes in the aesthetics underlying the *raga* system.

Many Sanskrit treatises including the *Raga Darpana, Sangita Darpana, Sangita Parijata,* and Hindi treatises such as *Man Kutuhala* were made available in Persian for the benefit of a group of connoisseurs ignorant of the Hindi dialects. It is interesting to note that the descriptions of the distinctive images (*tasvir*) of the *ragas* were demanded in Persian versions. A study of the text containing the Persian versions of *Ragamala* pictures shows that although the identity of the characteristics of each *raga* is adhered to in the interpretations, a good deal of the romantic atmosphere and mystical significance inherent in Hindi love-poetry, derived from the *rasa-shastra* (canons of erotics) is missing in the Persian translations, though an element of glamour is still retained in the illustrations.[12]

Raga-rasa as expounded in modern works

Musicological texts written later than the second half of the nineteenth century present diverse views about the *rasa* doctrine being applied to music in general and to *raga* in particular. Bharata's arbitrary statement regarding a specific *rasa* to be associated with a particular *svara, jati* and so on without elaborating the relevant logic, has raised many questions. The different views expressed by modern writers can be broadly classified into four categories. (1) Authors who subscribe to the traditional theory of *rasa* as it is found in *Natyashastra,* without attempting any kind of modifications to link it with the *raga* concept of the contemporary period. (2) Authors who have taken a step ahead and tried to provide an independent explanation either supporting or contradicting the *raga-rasa* association. (3) Authors who have attempted to present scientific explanations of a theoretical nature for the *raga-rasa* relation by drawing upon the principles of modern psychology, physiology and physics. (4) Authors who have adopted empirical methods to investigate the effect of music on human psychology, focusing on *rasa* theory in music.

Proponents of traditional rasa theory

While dealing with Indian music, authors such as H.A. Popley in *The Music of India,*[13] Peggy Holroyde in *Indian Music,*[14] and Mani Sahukar in *The Appeal in Indian Music*[15] have placed emphasis on the concept of *rasa* in Indian music. Definite statements are made indicating the association of a particular *raga* with a specific *rasa.* H.A. Popley points out that *ragas* depicting sadness have an average of three flats as against an average of two flats in *ragas* associated with joyous emotions.[16] Peggy Holroyde observes that a single note in isolation cannot express a specified sentiment; rather it is the way a certain note is used, its duration and expression in combination with the ornamentation of graces that can influence the mind.[17]

Writers such as Antsher Lobo in his article 'Multiple functions of *Vadi* and *Samvadi*' (1957), Ram Avtar Vir in *Theory of Indian Music* (1980) and Bishen Swarup in *Theory of Indian Music* (1950), have preferred to dwell upon the conventional aspects of *rasa* theory in music, viz. *rasa* related to *shrutis, shruti-jatis, svaras* and *jatis.* All of them unilaterally uphold Bharata's principle of *amsha (vadi) svara* being the controlling factor in deciding the *rasa* of a *raga.* Antsher Lobo argues that, if the position of *vadi svara* is altered in a particular *raga,* a definite change is observed with respect to the resultant emotion. Further, he specifies the emotive effect of certain note combinations.[18] For example, the combination of *Panchama* and *Shadja* results in a joyous mood which is expressive of sunshine or *Madhyama* and *Shadja* when combined produce a subdued effect of peace and so on. However, these associations, as well as the illustrations offered to prove the change in mood due to a shift in the *vadi* note, have not been supported by scientific explanations, and hence do not seem convincing.

In an attempt to provide a justification for the practice of associating a specific *rasa* with a particular *raga,* Ram Avatar Vir gives an example of *raga Asavari.*[19] However, the statements describing the emotive value of the *raga Asavari* are very arbitrary and hence the attempted explanation sounds capricious, e.g. "...in ascent, she (the main character of the *raga Asavari* is presumed to be a female) is full of joy, eagerness, hence tries to proceed ahead in very swift steps leaving and overlapping several notes behind..." or "...descent is not as encouraging and hopeful as ascent was..., so in a very slow and silent manner (she) steps on Sa, Ni, Dha and stops at Pa...etc."[20]

Bishen Swarup too resorts to questionable statements such as, "In the case of Bhupali, Ga (*gandhar*) is vadi which shows anger, and Dha (*dhaivat*) is *samvadi* showing worry, Re (*rishabh*) and Pa (*pancham*) near Ga excite admiration, love and soften down anger, while Sa (*shadja*) brings calmness. There is no bitterness because Ni (*nishad*) is absent."[21]

Thakur Jaideva Singh in his article 'The Concept of *Rasa*' chooses to present the *rasa* doctrine as expounded by Bharata and other rhetoricians. However, without entering into the debatable issue of specificity of *raga-rasa* he concludes that when a musician becomes *tanmaya* or one with the spirit of the *raga*, the *rasa* experienced is always of *ananda* or eternal bliss.[22]

Authors presenting subjective opinions about raga-rasa

Writers in this category have pointed out certain limitations in applying Bharata's *rasa* theory to the concept of *raga*, especially in the context of the contemporary music scene. Some of them have provided an independent basis for justifying the *raga-rasa* relation, while a few have questioned the very existence of the *raga-rasa* association.

G.S. Tembe in his article *'Raga* and *Rasa'*[23] supports the idea of notes (tones) bearing the latent power of producing an aesthetic effect. He insists that notes alone contribute to the *rasa* creation. Without providing any rationale, he attaches the following emotional attributes to different notes.[24] These types of highly subjective associations cannot be accepted in the present context unless they are subjected to scientific scrutiny. Until such a time they remain as vague as the similar associations proposed by Bharata regarding the individual notes and their *rasas* in the ancient period.

To end the discussion on notes and corresponding emotional effects, Tembe asserts that these qualities of the *svaras*

TABLE 7

Emotional attributes of notes according to G.S. Tembe

Notes	*Emotional attribute*
Shadja	like a *yogi* beyond any attachment
Rishabha (komala)	rather sluggish
Rishabha (shuddha)	reminding of indolence of a person waking up from sleep
Gandhara (komala)	bewildered, helpless and pitiable
Gandhara (shuddha)	fresh and pleasant
Madhyama (shuddha)	grave, noble and powerful
Madhyama (tivra)	sensitive, luxurious
Panchama	brilliant, self-composing
Dhaivata (komala)	grief, pathos
Dhaivata (shuddha)	robust, lustful
Nishada (komala)	gentle, happy, affectionate
Nishada (shuddha)	piercing appeal

ultimately depend on their tonal contexts.[25] Making the bold statement that the "sentiment of a *rasa* is self-existent irrespective of the musician or the audience", he proposes the usefulness of only four *rasas,* viz., the pathetic (*Karuna*), beatific (*Shanta*), erotic (*Shringara*) and heroic (*Vira*), for the purpose of music.[26] Subscribing to the traditional principle of *vadi svara* being the determinant factor in producing a specific *rasa,* he hypothesizes that when *Shuddha madhyama* is made to dominate a melody, it leads to a serene and sublime atmosphere, e.g., *ragas* such as *Malkauns, Lalita, Bageshri, Kedara,* etc. Yet, when *Panchama* assumes the dominant position, an invigorating and erotic effect is experienced.[27]

Citing specific examples of renowned performers, Chetan Karnani in *Listening to Hindustani Music* reports a disparity between the traditionally prescribed *rasa* of a *raga* and that actually experienced by the listeners.[28] He also observes an inconsistency regarding the nature of the *rasa* experienced and concludes that since a *raga* represents a complex set of feelings, a simple equation specifying a particular *rasa* for a given *raga,* cannot be prescribed.

S.N. Ratanjankar, a well-known musician and musicologist of this century, in his article 'Individual Notes and Specific *Rasas*' maintains that the individual notes may be pleasing but they cannot be associated with any specific emotion.[29] He theorizes that although the individual notes have no meaning, the appropriate context can lead to meaningful expressions. Presenting a revolutionary thought, the author states, "to me *rasa* conveys an abnormal state of mind".[30] According to the author, music is an expression of the soul, and the effect of music is holy communion with the soul.[31] The significance of melodic context in creating appropriate emotional expression, as recognised by this author, is relevant in the present study because the effect of varying melodic contexts upon the intonation of individual notes has been studied.

In his *The Filigree in Sound,* Gopal Sharman tries to have a dual view. On one hand he emphasizes that Indian music should not be evaluated as representing a specific emotion only, while on the other hand, he unhesitatingly puts forward certain statements linking notes and *ragas* with a specific emotional character.[32] For instance, the domination of *Shuddha rishbha, Dhaivata* and *Gandhara* is said to produce a romantic sentiment, or heroic emotion is said to be portrayed through *ragas* showing dominance of *Komala gandhara* and *Nishada.* Further, there are statements such as, "*Yaman raga* brings forth pensive mood because of use of *tivra madhyam,* though use of *shuddha rishabh, dhaivat, gandhar* lend romantic overtones...."[33]

In response to a query pertaining to the relation between notes, *ragas* and *rasa,* Pandit V.N. Bhatkhande in his work *Hindustani Sangeet Paddhati,* vol. IV, highlights the antiquity of Bharata's aphorism regarding *rasas* of the individual notes.[34]

TABLE 8

Relation of *ragas* and *rasas* according to Bhatkhande

(a) *Sandhiprakasha ragas*	—	*Karuna* and *Shanta rasa*
(b) *Ragas* employing *Shuddha rishabha, Dhaivata* and *Gandhara*	—	*Shringara rasa*
(c) *Ragas* employing *Komala Dhaivata* and *Nishada*	—	*Vira rasa*

Explaining the inadequacy of *vadi svara* in determining the *rasa* of *ragas,* he suggests the above classification. However, he hastily adds that these are mere suggestions which need to be thoughtfully examined. This author is quite justified in questioning the validity of Bharata's theory of relating *rasas* with individual notes and further, he realises the need for an objective assessment of his views on *raga* and *rasa.*

Various handbooks written for the purpose of introducing new students to the academic study of music, mention a specific *rasa* for individual *ragas.*[35] Nowhere is a detailed discussion attempted about *rasa,* but *rasa* is mentioned under a stereotype description of the *raga,* e.g., *Malhara raga—Karuna, Shringara rasas*[36] or *Puriya—Shringara; Bhupali—Shanta rasa.*[37]

It is interesting to note that Raghava Menon in *The Sound of Indian Music* has suggested that the audience who presumes a specific *rasa* to be associated with a particular *raga* may perceive the same *rasa*, intensely.[38] Instead of giving specifications relating a *raga* and a specific *rasa*, he prefers to give generalised statements such as, "There are some (kind of *ragas*) that give you a feeling of festivity.... There are some that may give you a feeling of April, *Holi* or *Baisakhi* or *ragas* that seem to give you the musical equivalent of *champa* or *jasmine....*"[39]

Providing a detailed analysis of the excerpts relating to the music from *Abhijnanashakuntala* and *Malavikagnimitra*, K.P. Jog in his article 'Some concepts in ancient Indian aesthetics' supports the theory of certain notes and *ragas* being associated with specific *rasas*.[40] Further he rightly observes that today, creative artists have defied the conventions regarding *raga-rasa*.[41]

After describing the details of Bharata's *rasa* theory and its application to music, Swami Prajnanananda in *Music of South-Asian Peoples* goes on to define musical tones as energized particles in vibration.[42] Seeking the help of principles of modern nuclear physics and psychology, he attempts to project a relationship between the seven musical tones and the seven colours.[43] He concludes that the musical tones are living and full of energy, hence they can constitute a living and dynamic melodic form.[44]

In an attempt to retrieve the connection between *raga* and *rasa*, the well-known musician and musicologist, late Pandit Onkarnath Thakur used to deliver a short speech about the *raga* to be performed, with a view to provide a definite orientation towards the emotive content of the *raga*. As a staunch follower of the *shruti* theory in music, this great musician in his works *Pranavabharati* and *Sangitanjali* cites the following relationship of five states of mind with the five *shruti-jatis* as described by Shri Roop Goswami in *Vaishnava Rasa-shastra*.[45]

To illustrate the significance of the precise *shruti* for bringing forth the appropriate kind of emotion, the author's own experience with *raga Todi* is narrated.[46] Explaining the effects of different notes on human physiology, suggestions are given to experimentally verify these effects in combination with the psychological effects.[47] In addition to *shrutis,* the author also elaborates other factors influencing *rasa* such as *svarantara* (note intervals), *svara-kaku* (tonal modulations), *svara-sangati* (melodic phrases), *saptaka-bheda* (different registers), *tala* (rhythm), and *laya* (tempo).[48] The following illustrations are provided to elucidate the relationship between

TABLE 9
Association of *rasa* with *shruti-jatis*

Rasas	*Shruti-jatis*
Shanta	*madhya*
Dasya, Sakhya, Vatsalya	*mridu*
Vira, Adbhuta	*ayata*
Karuna, Raudra, Bibhatsa,	*dipta*
Bhayanaka	*karuna*

the tone-interval and mood: *Komala gandhara* and *Tivra madhyama* in *Hindola* brings *tivrata,* whereas the same *Madhyama* accompanied by *Shuddha madhyama* creates *mridutva;*[49] in *raga Shri, Komal rishabha* with *Panchama* is emphasized to produce *Bhayanaka* and *Bibhatsa rasas.*[50] Yet some other specifications offered by the author are as follows:

1. *Ragas* which have movement in higher octaves exhibit the *Vira rasa,* e.g. *Shankara, Adana, Hindola,* etc.[51]
2. *Ragas* which predominantly employ *Shadja-madhyama samvad* (interval of fourth) bring out *shanta* and a serious mood, e.g., *Kedara, Bhinna-shadja, Malkauns,* etc.
3. *Ragas* without a very definite mode of movement represent the *Shringara rasa,* e.g., *Khamaj, Jhinjhoti, Pahadi, Mand,* etc.
4. *Ragas* which employ *Komala dhaivata* along with *Shuddha madhyama* portray the *Karuna rasa,* e.g., *Jogia, Gauri,* etc.[52]

In attempting to describe various *ragas*, the author seems to have favoured the expression *prakriti* (nature or character) to denote the emotional content. Also, the attributes used for denoting *prakriti* are not necessarily the ones used by Bharata and his followers.[53] In his lecture series on *raga* and *rasa* the author observes that even in the absence of *sahitya* (text), *svaras* are self-sufficient for the expression of *rasa*.[54] Practical demonstrations of the following *ragas* are provided with a view to illustrate the corresponding *rasas*: *Bhairava—Bhayanaka, Raudra; Jogia—Karuna; Bageshri—Viraha, Karuna; Todi—Viraha; Kambhoji—Shringara* and so on.[55] As a concluding remark the author states that his views about *raga-rasa* are entirely based on contemporary music practice. Although the associations proposed here are not entirely without subjectivity, they are important observations based not only on theoretical norms but also on actual practical experiences.

In collaboration with the great Ustad Abdul Karim Khan, his disciple Pandit Balkrishnabuva Kapileshwari carried out research on the *shruti-svara* relationship with respect to many *ragas*. Although the entire process is of a speculative nature, the author in his work *Shruti-darshan* concludes that a *shruti-svara* cannot bring forth the appropriate *rasa* unless it is aided by *shabdartha*, or the semantics of the text.[56]

While enumerating *svara* (notes), *laya* (tempo) and *vani* (speech) as the essential ingredients of *rasa-paripaka (rasa-process)* in music, Acharya K.C.D. Brihaspati in his work *Bharata ka Sangita Siddhanta* attempts to specify *rasa* of a particular *mela* (parent scale) on the basis of its *jati* and *murchhana*.[57] He has attempted to connect *amsha-svara* (principal notes) with *sthayi-bhava* (basic emotion), *samvadi-svaras* (consonant notes) of the *amshas* with *uddipana-vibhava* (causes of emotion), *anuvadi-svaras* (associated notes) with *anubhavas* (effects) and the *sanchari-svaras* (specific combination of *svaras*) with the *sanchari-bhava* (contributory emotions). Thus, he has tried to re-establish Bharata's dictum of *amsha-svara* being the determinant of *rasa*. All the same, it is difficult to accept this theory in the context of present-day music unless a general consensus is evolved regarding the specificity of music-related concepts such as *vadi, samvadi, anuvadi svara,* etc.

Stating that *rasas* like *Hasya* (humorous), *Raudra* (furious) and *Bibhatsa* (odious) cannot be articulated through music, M.R. Gautam in *The Musical Heritage of India* suggests that it is the musical elements such as the *svaras* or notes, rhythm and *kaku-bheda* (the different articulated colourings of tone leading to the timbre dynamics) etc. which lead to the desired aesthetic effect of *rasa.*[58] In support of this statement, the author provides a discussion of *raga Bhairava.* The description of the *raga* is given in the form of *raga-dhyana,* and then an attempt is made to illustrate the traditionally indicated set of *rasas* for *raga Bhairava.* The author proposes strategies involving different note progressions, embellishments like *gamakas,* accentuated tempo and the text of the composition to realise three types of *rasa,* viz., *Shanta, Vira,* and *Adbhuta,* that are supposedly associated with *raga Bhairava.*[59]

Further, the author surmises that *rasas* like *Shanta, Karuna* and *Shringara* are musically similar to one another and it would be difficult to express them distinctly without the help of the words.[60] In addition, certain general attributes regarding the emotional content of *svaras* and their specific combinations are given. For example, *Komala rishabha, Dhaivata* and *Gandhara* would be indicative of *viraha* (separation), renunciation and *bhakti* (devotion). The association of *Shuddha* or *Antara gandhara, Shuddha rishabha* and *dhaivata* with *Shuddha madhyama* would depict the mood of *Shringara* and so on.[61] Although some of the statements are not substantiated, the author deserves credit for recognizing the significance of aspects such as timbre-dynamics, tempo, specific note progressions, embellishments, etc. in the experience of *rasa.* Some of these aspects are investigated in the present study.

Premlata Sharma, a well-known musicologist, in her articles on *raga* and *rasa* asserts that the description of *rasa* found in traditional treatises cannot be applied as it is to present-day music.[62] Pointing to the limitations of directly applying the parameters of the *rasa* theory that was developed in the context of drama to our music today, which has totally lost the context of drama, the author suggests that certain concepts from the '*dhvani* school' of poetry can be adopted to help establish a rationale for the relationship between musical elements and the particular *rasa*.[63] Further, she proposes three terms, viz., *madhurya guna, ojas guna* and *prasada guna* to logically categorize the abstract effect of musical representations.[64] Based on certain principles of aesthetic criticism, the logic developed by the author is noteworthy. Since the vagueness and abstract nature of musical representations can fit quite well into these broad-based terms, they are suitable not only to describe the aesthetic effect of a *raga* but also of any kind of musical expression.

Authors expressing views based on modern scientific principles

G.H. Ranade in his work *Hindustani Music: Its Physics and Aesthetics*, recognizes music as a dual entity. He points out that besides being an art, music is a science governed by certain physical laws, hence amenable to inquiry based on scientific principles.[65] The author underlines the need for eliminating subjective and groundless elements to arrive at a meaningful solution to the problem of *raga-rasa*.[66] The author advocates analysis of the 'note-tonic' relationship,[67] particularly that of the *vadi* (dominant) note of the scale. The consonance of the *vadi* note with the tonic is supposed to have a gay and bright effect, whereas, dissonance is said to create a sad and dull effect. In addition, a medial type of consonance is reported to have neither a bright nor a very dull effect.[68]

Apart from the individual note character, the significance of various tonal and rhythmic forms of expression for producing the desired emotional effect is recognized by the author.[69] Even though the approach adopted to study the problem of *rasa* appears to be theoretical in nature, this work has opened up a new dimension of scientific inquiry for resolving complex musical issues such as *raga-rasa*.

In an attempt to justify the notion that music creates emotional effects, R.L. Batra in *Science and Art of Indian Music* states that auditory perceptions of music are converted by the 'music faculty' (situated in the brain) into impulses which finally take the form of 'emotions' and produce specific sensory and motor reactions.[70] The author claims that the above statement is made on the basis of certain verified scientific principles.[71] Speaking of Indian music, he presents a list of the emotional effects assigned to each of the twenty-two *shrutis,*[72] (refer to Appendix 2). The author simply states that the names of *shrutis* are indicative of the emotional states that they induce. He neither provides the source of information nor the rationale for such an assumption. It is rather curious to note that the author attributes therapeutic value to music on the basis of its emotional content. Depending upon the *rasa* of music, its utility as a therapeutic agent is recognized by the author.[73]

Based on the principles of physiology, Prabhakar Padhye in his article 'Imagination weaves a rhythmic pattern of energy in art' develops a logic which he uses to oppose the theory of music being capable of eliciting emotional responses.[74] He argues that the state of mind produced by listening to music or by any other work of art, is not one of emotion (aesthetic or otherwise) but of a pure rise in the level of energy that lies at the root of consciousness.[75] This rise in energy level is said to manifest in a peculiar aesthetic poise.

Among the views of various scholars discussed so far, the above view seems to be very different. The author not only disapproves of the idea of a music-mood relationship but also opts to define the effect of music as causing a pure rise in the energy level.

Also drawing upon the principles of physiology, Bhavanrao Pingle in *History of Indian Music* observes that the voice is a transformtion or equivalent of the respiratory movement, useful as a means of expressing emotions.[76] Comparing speech and music, he maintains that muscular action is directly proportional to mental excitement and hence, musical tones are more sonorous than speech sounds.[77] He also observes that the frequency ratio of one sound to other is a determining cause of phenomena of consonance and dissonance.[78] Thus a general discussion on music and its pleasant effect is offered by this author without going into the controversial aspect of specificity of the effect.

Dr. Ashok Ranade, a well-known musician and musicologist, in his article 'Affective Analysis of North Indian *Ragas*' advocates a need for reviewing the methodological procedures adopted for resolving complex problems such as the meaning of music.[79] He maintains that the special characteristics of Indian music such as improvisation and oral tradition independent of a written score, make it distinct from western music. Thus it becomes necessary to reconsider the application of western methodology to analyse both physiological and psychological affective responses arising from Indian music. Stressing the importance of careful selection of an appropriate *raga* and the basic musical unit to be used (*cheez, aroha-avroha,* etc.) for understanding the mood-music problem, he declares that music has only two moods—a mood of elation and one of dejection.[80] Further, he asserts that a conclusive statement about the intrinsic relationship between music and mood is possible only up to a certain point. Beyond that, individual associations may lead to sub-grouping and defy a general statement.[81] In the present context, we may be able to accept this view up to a certain point. In order to overcome the problems associated with the statements indicating specificity of moods, this strategy of broad-based description may seem suitable. At the same time, the total elimination of sub-grouping may well be inadequate for describing the music-mood relationship. Hence, an optimum level of categorization may seem to be the order of the day!

Ashok Kelkar, a linguist and philosopher, in his paper 'Understanding Music and the Scope for Psychological Probes' considers the possibility of a 'modern' restatement of *rasa* in music.[82] While disapproving of a simple one-to-one correspondence between the musical phrases and moods, he admits that there is some relationship between the two. In order to understand this relationship, the author proposes a psychological inquiry probing many aspects such as (i) the role of individual notes, the sequence of notes, the whole musical piece and *tala,* (ii) the relationship between the dominant *rasa* of a piece and the passing moods in the course of its performance, (iii) the significance of traditional associations between various musical elements and specific moods, and (iv) the role of the audience in the *rasa* process.[83]

In her article 'Conceptual Framework for Analysis of Aesthetic Behaviour', the well-known psychologist Shyamala Vanarase suggests a conceptual frame including context, stimulus, organism and response for enabling the psychological analysis of aesthetic behaviour.[84]

The models proposed by the last two authors for studying the problem of music and mood in a scientific manner deserve consideration. Experiments can be designed to incorporate the suggestions made by these psychologists for conducting an empirical study.

Authors adopting empirical approaches to examine the mood-music relationship

In recent times, some empirical studies have been carried out in order to understand the effect of sound (in speech and in music) upon human psychology and physiology. But with reference to the *raga-rasa* issue in Indian music, very few studies have been reported. The following are the accounts of two such endeavours:

Prof. B.C. Deva is one of those pioneering modern scholars who have attempted to undertake an empirical study to probe into some of the complex problems of musicology. In his work *Music of India: A Scientific Study* he observes that although music is fundamentally a non-referential form of art, we are affected by music and it can certainly excite us.[85] Further, he emphasizes that music does not express a particular emotion but creates certain parallel states of mind.[86] Statements regarding a particular *raga* or a note creating a particular emotion are regarded by the author as personal and highly individualized conclusions, not borne out of empirical examination.[87] In collaboration with K.G. Virmani, the author conducted several investigations to study the psychological responses of nearly 230 respondents to a few *ragas* of Indian music, including *Kafi, Misra Manda, Puriya-Dhanasri, Ragesri, Bhairava, Asavari (Komala rishabha), Bhairavi, Khamaj, Marva, Todi,* and *Yaman.* Employing the technique of Osgood's 'semantic differential scale' for quantifying the nature of moods aroused by the musical excerpts, the authors aimed at comparing the mood 'created' with the mood 'intended' by the *ragas* used as stimuli.

In conclusion it is reported that the mood of the *raga* is described better verbally (the adjectives used were different from the traditionally specified *rasas*). When an attempt was made to relate *rasas* to *ragas,* the results were much less definite in comparison with traditional descriptions.[88] The results obtained by this study may not be very conclusive, yet this endeavour has heralded a new era of empirical study in Indian musicology.

K.R. Rajgopalan and M. Chandrasekharan have reported a similar study with respect to Karnataka music in an article 'Appeal of Karnataka Music'.[89] The study was designed to detect differences in the emotions created in subjects who are aware of the intricacies of a particular music and in subjects who are not generally exposed to that particular music. The audience response to excerpts played from six Karnataka *ragas* (instrumental music only) was quantified using a scaled list of twenty-six bi-polar adjectives. The authors report that a conclusive statement regarding the 'mood' or 'aspect' of an experience cannot be made using such a large list of adjectives.[90]

The perusal of the various viewpoints regarding *raga-rasa* presented in this chapter makes it evident that this age-old concept is still prevalent in the minds of a few performers and musicologists of Indian music. This concept of *rasa* enumerated by Bharata, with a simple *sutra* (aphorism):

*"tatra vibhavanubhava vyabhicharibhavadrasanishpattih"**
(VI, text following v. 31),

has been commented upon by later Sanskrit scholars in different ways. However, even today, we do not have any conclusive statement about the *raga-rasa* theory using empirical research.

In the present work an attempt has been made to study *raga-rasa* in an acoustical perspective, which has produced concrete evidence regarding the *rasa* theory in *raga* exposition. An acoustical examination of the intonation of the notes and their melodic movements reveals that there is a definite similarity regarding these aspects in a performance of a given *raga* by different vocalists. This suggests a correlation between the tonal configuration of the *raga* and its aesthetic effect.

References

1. Premlata Sharma, 'Raga Theory and Indian Music', in *Sangeet Natak*, journal of Sangeet Natak Akademi, p. 61.
2. R.K. Shringy and Premlata Sharma, trs., *Sangita Ratnakara*, vol. I, p. 159.
3. *Brihaddeshi*, Trivandrum Sanskrit Series edn., p. 87.
4. O.C. Gangoly, *Raga-s and Ragini-s*, p. 19.
5. *Sangita Makaranda*, p. 19.
6. R.K. Shringy and Premlata Sharma, trs., op. cit., vol. I, pp. 138-40.
7. *Kitab-i-Nauras*, p. 56.
8. Shubhankara, *Sangita Damodara*, pp. 36-41.
9. *Chatvarinsatchata Raganirupanam*, p. 13.
10. O.C. Gangoly, op. cit., pp. 115-17.
11. Ibid., p. 132.
12. Ibid., p. 143.
13. p. 64.
14. pp. 158-63.
15. p. 39.
16. Popley, p. 65.
17. Holroyde, p. 160.
18. Antsher Lobo, in *Aspects of Indian Music*, p. 49.

*"Now, *rasa* arises from a (proper) combination of *vibhava* (stimulants), *anubhava* (consequent) and *vyabhichari bhava* (transient emotional states)."

19. Ram Avatar, *The Theory of Indian Music*, p. 130.
20. Ibid.
21. Bishen Swarup, *The Theory of Indian Music*, p. 187.
22. Thakur Jaidev Singh, in *Aspects of Indian Music*, p. 61.
23. G.S. Tembe, in *Aspects of Indian Music*, p. 20.
24. Ibid, pp. 21-22.
25. Ibid., p. 23.
26. Ibid., p. 24.
27. Ibid., p. 25.
28. *Listening to Hindustani Music*, p. 52.
29. S.N. Ratanjankar, in *Aspects of Indian Music*, p. 55.
30. Ibid., p. 57.
31. Ibid., p. 58.
32. Gopal Sharman, *The Filigree in Sound*, p. 66.
33. Ibid.
34. *Hindustani Sangita Paddhati*, vol. IV, p. 25.
35. Patwardhan, *Raga-Vidnyan* and Rajopadhye, *Sangitashastra.*
36. Patwardhan, *Raga-Vidnyan*, p. 16.
37. Rajopadhye's Appendix in *Sangitashastra.*
38. *The Sound of Indian Music*, p. 21.
39. Ibid.
40. K.P. Jog, in *Psychology of Music*, p. 84.
41. Ibid.
42. *Music of South-Asian Peoples*, p. 61.
43. Ibid., p. 62.
44. Ibid., p. 64.
45. Onkarnath Thakur, *Pranavabharati*, p. 54.
46. Ibid., p. 46.
47. Ibid., p. 34.
48. Ibid., p. 213.
49. Ibid., p. 51.
50. Ibid., p. 203.
51. Onkarnath Thakur, *Sangitanjali*, vol. III, p. 14.
52. Ibid., p. 15.
53. Vide *Sangitanjali*, vol. 5.
54. Onkarnath Thakur, *Raga ane Rasa*, pp. 44-49.
55. Ibid., pp. 52-64.
56. Balkrishna Kapileshwari, *Shruti-darshan*, p. 452.
57. K.C.D. Brihaspati's Appendix III in *Bharata ka Sangita Siddhanta.*
58. M.R. Gautam, *The Musical Heritage of India*, p. 65.
59. Ibid., p. 66.
60. Ibid., p. 67.
61. Ibid.

62. Premlata Sharma, 'Rasa Theory and Indian Music,' op. cit., p. 63; 'Raga and Rasa', *Report of Twelfth Congress of the International Musicological Society,* p. 528.
63. 'Raga and Rasa', op. cit., p. 529.
64. 'Rasa Theory and Indian Music', op. cit., p. 63; 'Raga and Rasa', op. cit., p. 530.
65. G.H. Ranade, *Hindustani Music: Its Physics and Aesthetics,* p. 26.
66. Ibid., p. 130.
67. Ibid., p. 131.
68. Ibid., p. 133.
69. Ibid., p. 137.
70. R.L. Batra, *Science and Art of Indian Music,* p. 11.
71. Ibid.
72. Ibid., pp. 19-20.
73. Ibid., p. 56.
74. *Psychology of Music,* p. 88.
75. Ibid.
76. Bhavanrao Pingle, *History of Indian Music,* p. 10.
77. Ibid., p. 14.
78. Ibid., p. 76.
79. Ashok Ranade, in *Psychology of Music,* p. 18.
80. Ibid., p. 21.
81. Ibid.
82. Ashok Kelkar, in *Psychology of Music,* p. 11.
83. Ibid., p. 12.
84. Shyamala Vanarase, in *Psychology of Music,* p. 28.
85. B.C. Deva, *Music of India: A Scientific Study,* p. 139.
86. Ibid., p. 140.
87. Ibid.
88. Ibid., p. 184.
89. Rajgopalan and Chandrasekharan, in *Studies in Musicology,* p. 141.
90. Ibid., p. 144.

CHAPTER 3

Indian and Western Interpretations on Rasa-Emotion

The concept of *rasa* that constitutes an essential aspect of *natya* or *drama*, has been borrowed from the *Atharvaveda* (*Natyashastra,* 1-7). In ancient times, music being an inseparable ingredient of *natya,* Bharata elaborately discussed *svaras* (notes), *jatis* (the ancient modal patterns) and *jati*-based *dhruvas* (the vocal compositions) with respect to their association with a specific *rasa.* Later, when the *raga* concept replaced the earlier *jati*-system, the *jati-rasa* relation as enunciated by Bharata was directly applied to *raga* and thus the *raga-rasa* relationship came into existence. Even when music became independent of drama proper, the relation of *raga* and *rasa* continued to be an integral element of the art of music.

In modern scientific usage, the term emotion has multi-dimensional referents that include: verbally expressible subjective experience, concomitant internal physiological changes and observable motor behaviour such as facial expression, gesture, posture etc.[1] 'Affect' is frequently used as a synonym for emotion and similar considerations apply to the concept of sentiment, feeling and mood.[2]

According to Leonard Meyer, a well-known composer, critic and aesthetician of music, 'musical mood gestures' may be similar to 'behavioural mood gestures' since both, the emotional behaviour and music involve motions differentiated by the same qualities such as energy, directions, tension, continuity and so forth.[3] Further, he adds, "because moods and sentiments attain their most precise articulation through vocal inflection, it is possible for music to imitate the sounds of emotional behaviour with same precision." However, he points out that since musically affective stimuli are obviously different from the referential stimuli of real life, there will always be a generic difference between musical affective experience and the experience of everyday life, and hence musical experience is unique.[4]

Authors between the time of Bharata (200 BC–AD 200) and Sharngadeva (thirteenth century AD) attributed a particular *rasa* to the *amsha svara* (principal note) of a *jati* or *raga.* A number of later authors have merely repeated the classical theory of *rasa* as expounded in the *Natyashastra* without making any kind of effort to link it with the contemporary performing practice of a *raga.* A few others have attempted to provide intuitive explanations either supporting or contradicting the *raga-rasa* association. Another school of modern thinkers has attempted to present a scientific explanation for the *raga-rasa* relationship by drawing on the principles of interdisciplinary approach. However, these endeavours are of a theoretical nature and need to be experimentally verified. Recently, some empirical approaches have been made towards investigating the effect of sound (in speech and in music) upon human psychology and physiology.[5] There have been only a few isolated studies of this nature, and hence their findings remain more or less inconclusive regarding the complex issue of *raga-rasa.*

Since the very idea of *rasa* is unique to Indian poetics and dramatics, there is no single equivalent term in western language which can convey its complete import. However, the concept itself may have a semblance to *ethos* in ancient Greece or to the similar phenomenon of *affektenlehre* of the late eighteenth century[6] or to a little extent it may appear similar to the idea of *duende* prevalent in Spanish Flamenco dance. The German expression *eurfulung* or modern English word 'empathy', both meaning 'feeling into', may be considered synonymous with the concept of *rasa.* Western philosophers have preferred various expressions such as ideal beauty, aesthetic relish, aesthetic sentiment, mood, emotional appeal, aesthetic *gestalt,* aesthetic experience, mental atmosphere and so on, to signify the concept of *rasa.*

Western views on music-emotion

There is an extensive body of literature available, comprising the diverse views expressed by numerous musicians, musicologists and psychologists from the time of Plato and Aristotle. However, as observed by Dr. Keller, it is only since Romanticism that the idea of music as a sonic artifact capable of emotional gratification has taken root in the West. The ideology of 'art for art's sake' could be nurtured only after it was disengaged from religion.[7] The available data implies that there seem to be two distinct groups of thinkers. One of them suggests that music is unable to imply anything that has worldly significance, while the other group maintains that music is the language of soul and is very much capable of arousing emotions. The former group of autonomists characterizes the effect of music as an aesthetic emotion which is far removed from the sphere of bodily sensations, while the latter group emphasizes the power of musical expressions to affect the human psyche.

The Greeks viewed the world of music as the ultimate and the greatest revelation of 'Being', the emanation of all creative cosmic force. For Plato (427-348 BC), the propounder of the Mimesis theory, music was dangerous and deserved to be censored, to prevent the people from indulging in immoral activities. His elaborations regarding the characteristic qualities of various modes bring out some interesting view-points. He suggested that the Lydian mode and Ionian mode expressing sorrow and self-indulgence be banned from his 'Ideal-Republic'. Plato associated the Dorian and Phrygian modes with courage, military spirit and endurance.

Aristotle (384-322 BC), a disciple of Plato, asserted that the function of art is not merely an imitation of nature but a rather consummation of what nature has left unfinished. He firmly regarded music as significant of life values and as capable of stimulating one's affective responses.[8] Homer, Euripides and other ancient Greeks attributed qualities such as amusement and relaxation to music.

Contradicting Aristotle, the first century philosopher Epicurean Philodemus opined that music is irrational and cannot affect the soul or the emotions. For Helmholtz and Comte, music was merely a source of pleasure. The modern key of C major condemned by Plato, was associated with brightness and strength by Helmholtz, while Ernst Pauer, in the English translation of Helmholtz's *Tonempfindungen,* suggests that the major mode is linked with purity, innocence, manliness and other virtues.

Rousseau and other music critics such as Riemann, great musicians like Beethoven, Schumann and Liszt, all believed the essence of music to be 'self-expression'. The French philosopher Rene Descartes (1596-1650) very closely apprehended the idea that music seeks to stimulate affective responses.[9] Proponents of the positive viewpoints have, as Liszt and Wagner did, held that music expresses different emotional states. Some, like Smetna and Strauss have pointed out that music also refers to actions and scenes from life.[10] For instance, the first movement of Mahler's 'Sixth Symphony' includes the cowbell episode which produces a realistic impression of the sound of a distant herd of cattle grazing in Alpine pastures.[11] As explained by Copland, a composer writes music to express, communicate and to put down in permanent form certain thoughts, emotions and states of being.[12]

Perusal of the literature pertaining to the history of aesthetics, and other informatory sources such as letters or personal communications providing composers' comments, may lead one to believe that philosophers and composers such as Mozart and Tschaikowsky intentionally tried to project extrinsic things, extrageneric objects and events through their compositions. Mozart, for example, in a letter to his father (August 26, 1781), speaks of extrageneric objects and events as emotional rage, a throbbing heart, whispering, sighing, etc. being signified during some of the passages in his opera, 'The Abduction from the Seraglio'.[13] Arthur Schopenhauer (1788-1860) supported this view of significant intentional connotation of the melody.

Immanuel Kant (1724-1804) agreed that music is a language of communicable affections but emphasized that the aesthetic ideas inherent in a piece of music are not concepts or determinate thoughts. It is curious to note that Kant had the bizarre idea of associating music and laughter, on account of the fact that both owe their origin to moods and emotive states. Herbert Spencer was the proponent of an emotionalistic theory and like Kant, he believed that music expresses through its tone and rhythm. Friedrich Hegel (1770-1831), from his heteronomist point of view, said that a work of art can awaken the most diverse and abstract sensibilities. He held that the effect of music proceeds to heart and inner self, and not to the intellectual realm.

Edward Hanslick (1825-1904) strongly refuted the theory of emotions being the substance of musical sounds. A staunch autonomist, he denied that music is a language of emotions[14] and declared that there is no link between music and nature. He insisted that beauty in music lies wholly in the content of the tone itself.[15]

Hanslick and other aestheticians after him ardently defended the point of view that the emotional side of music is non-aesthetic. They argued that, if the main goal of music is a direct emotional effect, then this removes it from the realm of aesthetics and it can be considered as a means of arousing emotive states. Hanslick argued that music cannot represent either thoughts, definite feelings or emotions. He maintained that music is an end in itself, not merely a means for the achievement of something to do with emotions.

In the modern period, Revesz has supported the view of Hanslick by stating, "Emotions are essentially different from musical configurations. The latter are not emotional experiences, but musical functioning wholes, and their forms are autonomous forms of musical expressions."[16] Further, he remarks that the effects of music are somehow different from real emotions. Carroll Pratt agreed with Revesz by contending that the tonal designs cannot be specifically related to emotion. Nonetheless, he emphasized that music sounds the way emotions feel.[17] Clarifying his standpoint, he added that these emotions are really not the ones experienced in actual life but are characteristics of the music and bear a striking formal resemblance to emotion.[18]

Igor Stravinsky (1882) rejected the idea that music is in any fundamental sense, expressive. He asserted that expression has never been an inherent element of music.[19] Contrary to this opinion, Mursell held that the material of music itself is a direct emotional stimulus of unique power. According to him, it sets up changes in the body, which are recognized at the physiological substrata of emotion.[20]

Carl Seashore, an eminent psychologist of the contemporary period, endorsed the opinion of Rousseau, Riemann, Liszt and others and believed music to be an emotional catharsis.[21] Susanne Langer, another modern psychologist, pointed out that if music has any significance it is semantic and not symptomatic.[22] She maintains that, what music can actually reflect is only the morphology of feeling.[23]

Other psychologists like Dr. W. Brown and M. Cambarieu joined Hanslick and other autonomists to declare that music is a unique thought and is not related to the ordinary emotions of life.[24] It is interesting to note that both Tagore and Rolland thought that emotion has no direct role in music, but that it does subtly contribute to the creation of significant form in the art of music.

There are a few thinkers who have emphasized the role of the listener. According to M. Ribot's doctrine of 'emotional theory', the listener experiences a kind of emotional reverberation when a musical pattern arouses the abstract emotional state hidden in him. Depending upon these associations the listener perceives his own images, ideas and emotions. On the same line, Revesz rationalized that a productive artist forms a musical idea that comes to him intuitively and if an aesthetically sensitive listener absorbs the idea so fashioned, then he is brought nearer to the art work.[25]

Wilson Coker theorized that the meaning of musical gesture is a set of resultants of the adjustive behaviour of the listener and the musical organism. The meaning emerges as a response to the stimulus of musical gesture.[26] He states that the extrageneric meaning of music results from the interaction of the listener and the music.[27]

Upon analysing the effect of music experienced by listeners, Carl Seashore reported that there is no one-to-one relationship between the music performed and the music experienced. He suggested that the listener may read a great deal more into the music than that was originally intended or actually presented.[28]

While providing an account of subjective evaluations regarding the emotional qualities of musical scale, James Jeans mentions that many pianists are convinced about their ability to put a vast amount of expression into the striking of a single note on the piano, and some of them even claim to be able to draw a whole gamut of emotions out of a single key.[29] Further, he has provided a list of notes and the corresponding emotional qualities attributed to each one of them as listed in 'Curwen's Standard Course of Lessons and Exercises in the Tonic Sol-fa Method'.[30]

Similarities and dissimilarities between the Indian and Western views

The idea of enjoining a specific emotional quality to individual notes is found in Bharata's *Natyashastra.* The following Table provides a comparison of the emotional attributes assigned by Bharata, with those suggested by some of the Western musicians.[31]

From this Table, we may infer that the Indian and Western views have some similarities in the idea of suggesting emotional attributes related to musical notes. According to the Indian view, *Shadja* evokes emotions of *Vira* (valour), *Raudra* (fury) and *Adbhuta* (wonder), whereas, the note Do

TABLE 10
Emotional attributes for musical notes

Notes (Indian)	*Rasas attributed by Bharata*	*Notes (Western)*	*Emotional attributes suggested by Western musicians*
Shadja	*Vira, Raudra, Adbhuta*	Do	strong, firm
Rishabha	*Vira, Raudra, Adbhuta*	Re	rousing, hopeful
Gandhara	*Karuna*	Mi	steady, calm
Madhyama	*Shringara, Hasya*	Fa	desolate, awe-inspiring
Panchama	*Shringara, Hasya*	So	grand, bright
Dhaivata	*Bibhatsa, Bhayanaka*	La	sad, weeping
Nishada	*Karuna*	Ti	piercing, sensitive

in Western music which is equivalent to *Shadja* of Indian music, is said to express 'strong' and 'firm' attitudes. The note *Rishabha* in Indian tradition is assigned feelings of *Vira* (valour), *Raudra* (fury) and *Adbhuta* or wonder. The Western equivalent of *Rishabha,* the note Re, is associated with a 'rousing' and 'hopeful' mood. The notes *Gandhara* and *Nishada* in Indian music are associated with *Karuna rasa* or the pathetic mood, whereas the Western equivalent of *Gandhara,* i.e., Mi, is suggested to evoke a steady and calm mood. The note Ti of Western music which corresponds to the *Nishada* of Indian music, is said to express 'piercing' and 'sensitive' effects. In the Indian view, *Panchama* is associated with *rasas* like the *Shringara* (amorous) and *Hasya* (humorous) *rasa,* while its Western equivalent note So is said to express grand and bright effects. *Bibhatsa* (repugnant) and *Bhayanaka* (horrific) moods are those associated with the note *Dhaivata* in Indian tradition. The corresponding note in Western music, i.e. La, is associated with a 'sad' and 'weeping' effect.

The *jati-rasa* relationship proposed by Bharata and propagated by his followers as the *raga-rasa* relationship, is conceptually similar to the idea of assigning specific moods to different modes, e.g., the Lydian and Ionian modes were associated with sorrow and self-indulgence, while the Dorian and Phrygian modes were associated with courage, military spirit and endurance, by Plato. Similarly, the major mode was linked with purity, manliness and other virtues by Ernst Pauer, and so on. In both the traditions, great changes have been observed over the centuries regarding the specific emotional attribute associated with a given melody.

According to the *rasa* theory related to music, the emotive power of a melody depends upon the *vadi* or the *amsha svara*. Greek melodies would also stress *messe* or the most salient note of the mode, in order to impart to melody the character of that particular mode. A device known as the 'pivotal centre', stressing a certain fixed note in the melody, is often used by Western composers to impart the desired emotional character to a melody, e.g., in the finale theme of his ninth choral symphony, Beethoven has stressed the third note while Franz Schubert has laid emphasis on the second note of the scale in his composition 'Ave Maria'.

Although Bharata had specified the relationship between *jati*-based vocal compositions (*dhruvas*) and their corresponding *rasa*, in the later period this association seems to have gone out of vogue. However, in Western music, many accounts of certain compositions or a particular movement of a composition of great masters being linked with a particular mood-effect are abundant. For example. Mozart's 'Masonic funeral music' is said to express a sense of loss, Elgar's 'Sospiri' is associated with profound sorrow and a feeling of irrevocable loss, Beethoven's first 'Rasoumovsky' string quartet is an expression of sadness, the opening of Mendelssohn's 'Italian Symphony' is imbued with *joie de vivre* or the prelude to Wagner's 'Tristan' and Isolde' is suffused with yearning and so on.

In some of the modern Western compositions such as 'The Seasons' (1941), 'Amores' (1943), Sonatas and Interludes (1946-48), composers such as John Cage have tried to create a specific mood according to the Indian *raga* system, but not based on any particular *raga*. The rhythmic structure of these works is also reminiscent of Indian music.

According to Aristotle, music is a component of 'tragedy' and it is employed as an instrument for dramatic success. This reminds one of Bharata's *Natyashastra,* in which the Gana type of music is said to enhance the dramatic effect.

The concept of *rasa* is often compared to Aristotle's principle of catharsis. These are no doubt related ideas, both seeking to explain that the aesthetic experience is always pleasurable. However, the principle of catharsis stops at pleasure, while the *rasa* experience signifies a higher level of *ananda* or bliss, transcending the ordinary state of pleasure.

The role played by a sympathetic observer or *sahridaya* in the process of the *rasa*-experience was highlighted by Bharata and his follower Abhinavagupta. In the Western tradition as well, philosophers such as Revesz, Coker, Seashore, and Ribot have echoed similar thoughts about the aesthetically sensitive listener. Although physically the element of 'observer' cannot be placed within the domain of any art form, being an element operative at the psychological level, its significance in the realm of art experience has been well recognised by philosophers at all times.

The phenomenon of the evocation of human passions, sentiments and feelings is explained by psychologists like M. Ribot by enunciating the doctrine of 'emotional memory'. However, a similar concept had been already proposed by Abhinavagupta who emphasized the significance of 'past experience' in the process of aesthetic contemplation or *rasanubhava.*

For Hanslick, music was "A vital spark of the divine fire", which is similar to the idea of *"Nadaswarupam param jyoti"*, stated by Shubhankara in *Sangita Damodara.*[32]

Thus, both in Indian and Western traditions, the issue of the potentiality of music to affect the human psyche has been of great concern over the centuries. Ancient philosophers like Bharata, Abhinavagupta, Plato, Aristotle, Confucius and many others as well as modern psychologists, composers and musicians have contemplated upon the problem of the potentiality of music to make an impact on the non-linguistic and linguistic layers of the subconscious. This shows that in an intuitive way the ability of music to interact with human behaviour has been recognised for a long time. A comparative study of the Western and Indian critical traditions reveals that there are significant points of contact between the two and this might support the view that the tendency or the behavioural pattern of human beings to respond to music, is universal.

To sum up, the following Tables give an idea of similar views expressed by Indian and Western scholars.

TABLE 11
The role of music in theatre

Bharata	Gana type of music to enhance the dramatic effect
Aristotle	Music as component of 'tragedy' and to be employed for dramatic success

TABLE 12
Nature of effect of music

Aristotle	Principle of catharsis—pleasure
Bharata	*rasa* experience—higher level of *ananda* or bliss transcending ordinary pleasure

TABLE 13
Melodies and moods

Indian tradition	*Non-Indian tradition*
jati *raga*	different modes
rasa	emotional effects
Shringara (amorous)	sorrow
Bibhatsa (repugnant)	military spirit
Hasya (humorous)	manliness
Bhayanaka (horrific)	self-indulgence
Karuna (pathetic)	courage
Adbhuta (wondrous)	purity
Vira (heroic)	endurance
Raudra (furious)	
Shanta (calm)	

TABLE 14
Characteristic features of melody and mood

Rasa theory	Emotive power of *jati* or *raga* depends upon *vadi* or the *amsha svara*
Greek tradition	Stress on *messe*—the salient note of the mode to evoke the character of the melody
Western tradition	'Pivotal centre' to express the desired emotional effect of the melody

TABLE 15
The role of a listener

Indian Tradition	
Bharata	A sympathetic listener or *sahridaya* is an essential aspect of the *'rasa* experience'
Abhinavagupta	Significance of 'past experience' in the process of *'rasanubhava'*
Western Tradition	
M. Ribot	'Emotional theory'—process of arousal of abstract emotional states into mood experience
Revesz	Aesthetically sensitive listener absorbs musical ideas put forth by the artist
Wilson Coker	The meaning of musical gesture results from the adjustive behaviour of the listener and the musical organism
Carl Seashore	No 'one to one' relationship between the music performed and music experienced. Listener capable of adding a great deal into music that is actually presented

REFERENCES

1. *Encyclopaedia Britannica,* vol. 6, p. 757.
2. Ibid.
3. Leonard Meyer, *Emotion and Meaning in Music,* p. 268.
4. Ibid., p. 267.
5. Deva, pp. 141-222; Rajgopalan and Chandrasekharan, pp. 142-43; Podosky, p. 157; Mursell, pp. 27-28.
6. Walter Kaufmann, *The Raga-s of North India,* p. 10.
7. Marcello Keller, in *International Journal of Music Education,* p. 7.
8. *Aristotle on the Art of Poetry,* p. 45.
9. Rene Descartes, *Compendium of Music,* p. 11.
10. Oliver Strunk, *Source Readings in Music History,* pp. 848-49.
11. Hans Redlich, ed., *Mahler Symphony, no 6. A Minor,* p. xxix.

12. Aaron Copland, in *New York Times Magazine*, p. 11.
13. Sam Morgenstern, ed., *Composers on Music*, pp. 80-83.
14. Edward Hanslick, *The Beautiful in Music*, p. ix.
15. Ibid., pp. 104-16.
16. Revesz, *Introduction to Psychology of Music*, p. 241.
17. Carroll Pratt, *Meaning of Music: A Study of Psychological Aesthetics*, pp. xiv-xxv.
18. Ibid., p. 200.
19. Igor Stravinsky, *Chronicles of My Life*, p. 91.
20. James Mursell, *Psychology of Music*, p. 29.
21. Carl Seashore, *Psychology of Music*, p. 174.
22. Susanne Langer, *Philosophy in a New Key*, p. 16.
23. Ibid., p. 193.
24. O.C. Gangoly, op. cit., pp. 137-38.
25. Revesz, op. cit., p. 244.
26. Wilson Coker, *Music and Meaning*, p. 23.
27. Ibid., p. 147.
28. Carl Seashore, op. cit., p. 382.
29. James Jeans, *Science and Music*, p. 98.
30. Ibid., p. 184.
31. Ibid.
32. Ch. II, p. 16.

CHAPTER 4

Approaches used to Study Raga-Rasa in the Acoustical Perspective

In Indian music once the performer makes a choice of *raga* to be rendered, it is presumed that he is bound by the traditionally prescribed set of rules that govern the exposition of the chosen *raga*. Within the limits of set principles, a performer has freedom to improvise and build total structure of the *raga* through various components known as *bandish* (composition), *alapa, bola, sargam,* and *tana.* A performer seeks to portray the personality of the *raga* by employing his knowledge, skill and creativity. In an effort to bring out an appropriate aesthetic atmosphere of the given *raga,* various melodic and rhythmic possibilities are explored. The continuous exposition of a given theme in myriad ways brings forth a characteristic atmosphere that becomes intensely hypnotic as the performer reaches the pinnacle of his artistic endeavour. This atmosphere, although seems to be dominated by a specific mood, may possess streaks of other moods as well. Being of transitory nature, these do not interfere with the dominant mood but can provide special lusture by way of contrast.

Various factors involved in a musical performance are represented in the chart below. The integrated effect of these factors lead to what is referred to as the aesthetic *gestalt* or the experience of *rasa* at the perceptible level.

The unique personality of the *raga* constitutes a major part of the total aesthetic experience, while the subjective factors such the performer, his *gharana* (school), style, context, time

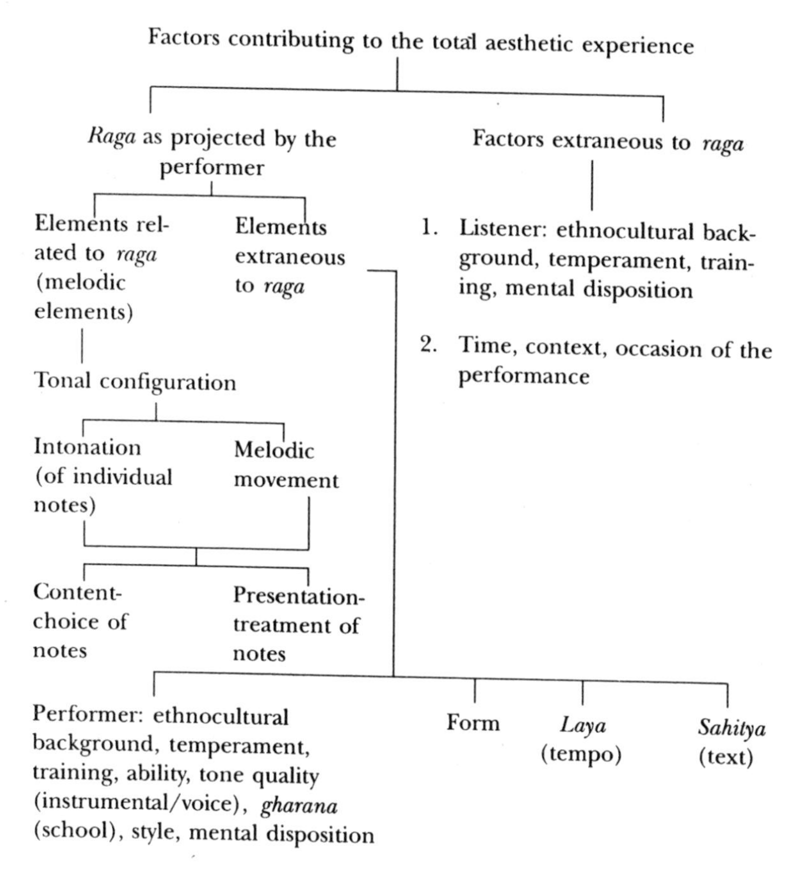

and occasion of the performance, mental and cultural background of listeners and performers etc. constitute the rest of the aesthetic experience. Elements related to principal tenets of *raga* remain unaltered, whereas, the subjective factors bring about the variance in a *raga*-performance. Further, the special elements associated with Indian classical music such as absence of a written score, oral transmission of knowledge and heavy dependence on improvisation, also add to the variability observed in a *raga*-performance. As a result, performances of the same *raga* by the same performer or by different performers at different occasions exhibit appreciable degree of divergence. In other words, the total performance is an interplay of the non-varying grammatical tenets of *raga* as well as the subjective factors.

However diverse are the ideas and viewpoints of musicologists be about *raga-rasa* relation (vide ch. 2), the fact that a *raga* projects a characteristic musical idea, resulting into a unique aesthetic atmosphere capable of arousing a neuro-psychological response, cannot be ruled out. Various aspects involved in a *raga* performance that lead to an aesthetic experience at the perceptible level, can be schematically represented as follows:

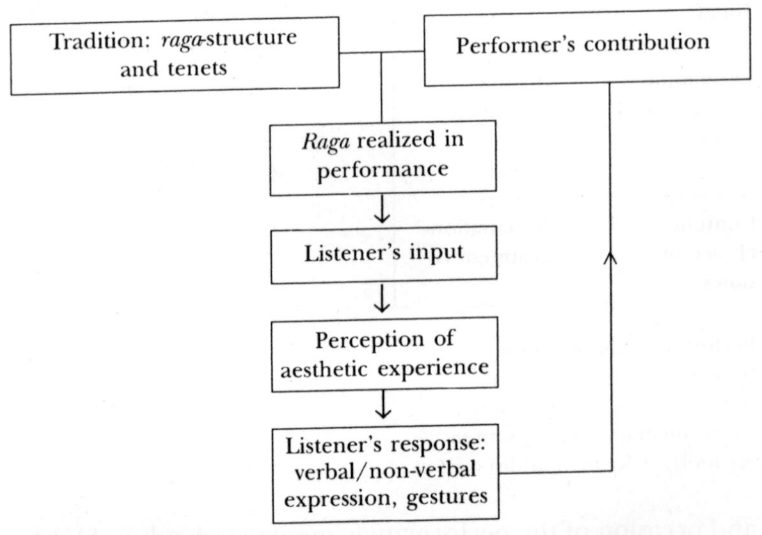

The codified set of rules of a *raga* are handed down by the tradition. Following these principles, the performer with his/her skill, training and ability, breathes life into the *raga* during a performance. The receptive listener receives at his level, the *raga*-image created by the performer. The aesthetic experience perceived by a listener, is really the synthesis of aesthetic ideas projected by the performer and his/her own aesthetic ideas. The listeners respond by exhibiting verbal and/or non-verbal expressions or gestures which in turn influence the performer and his creation. The Indian music tradition allows the listeners freedom for such an expression.

This means that the resultant aesthetic experience or the experience of *rasa* is a complex process involving many factors.

Therefore, even though traditionally every *raga* is assigned with a particular *rasa*, the subjectivity brought in by various factors may not allow to establish a consistent link between a *raga* and a specific *rasa*. Nonetheless, as experienced by the performers and connoisseurs of Indian music, a given *raga* is always projected with certain identity of its own, irrespective of the variables. This non-varying aesthetic identity of the *raga* is certainly due to the principles that govern its exposition and which are strictly followed by the performers in the course of a performance. The varying factors remain subjective, and are hence elusive to scrutiny. In the present study, an attempt is made to examine certain characteristics of a *raga* with a view to understand their contribution towards creating an aesthetic experience or the *rasa*.

As yet, only a few isolated experimental studies have been carried out to relate the psychological response of listeners to music stimuli, with a view to understand the *raga-rasa* relation (vide ch. 2). Generally such studies have assumed a simplistic model that could be applicable to any work of art. Schematic representation of the model is as follows:

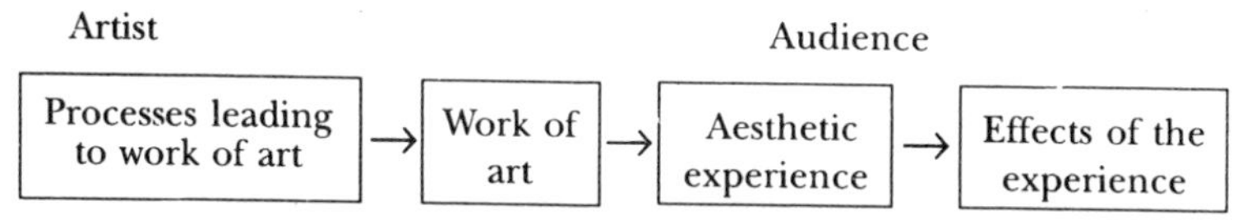

Schematic representation of the subject matter of aesthetics (adopted from Child-Irvine, 1969)

Such oversimplified model indicating unidirectional process obviously does not take account of the qualitative difference in performance brought out by the audience response. Further, the recorded versions of music-stimuli used in such studies are played out of the context of real performance in an artificial environment. This method may profoundly influence the audience response and hence introduce an element of non-reliability in the observations.

Besides, very little is known about the neurophysiological processes involved in the comprehension of musical messages. Nonetheless, music being a process that essentially presumes interaction of stimulus of sound with the response of listeners, such psycho-acoustical studies can indeed prove meaningful, provided proper methodology is adopted.

The problem of music-mood can also be viewed from the other end, that is to examine and analyze the source itself and to envisage those elements in music which bear potential to create an emotional response.

Music can be defined as an arrangement of, or the art of combining together, sounds that please the ear.[1] Being an organized structure of units of sound, music signals are communicated through acoustic waves and hence lend themselves to physical investigation. Like language, music provides evidence for a cognitive organization with a logic of its own. The musical path traversed by a performer is not of a random nature, but follows a logical direction involving organized pitch combinations leading to coherent patterns. The subjective characteristics of music such as pitch, loudness and timbre can be precisely quantified and evaluated using objective parameters of frequency, amplitude and harmonics respectively.

During the past few decades many powerful techniques of signal processing have been developed and are already being extensively used for the analysis and synthesis of speech. These instruments, techniques and software can be utilized for the study of musical sound, specially with a view to identify the important characteristics of this signal, which are responsible for lending emotional colour to music. In the present work, an attempt is made to conduct an acoustical study of some of the musical elements that have been traditionally accepted as factors influencing the creation of specific aesthetic atmosphere (see chart).

In India, a great deal of attention has been paid to 'pitch' in music. Bharata pioneered the concept of *shruti* or the microtones, which was elaborately dealt by many musicologists after him. The term *shruti* denotes an audible sound free from resonance and which is capable of being individually perceived, recognised and reproduced. Sharngadeva considered *shrutis* to be the factors manifesting *svaras* (*Sangita Ratnakara,* 1.3, 23). According to Sharngadeva as interpreted by Kallinatha, "*Shruti* signifies a pitch value which contributes to the musicality of tone and is yet by itself devoid of tonal colour."[2] The different notes are assigned with different *rasas* by Bharata. Further, *shrutis* have been distinguished in five classes viz., *dipta, ayata, mridu, madhya,* and *karuna.* Though the basis for such classification is not clear, comments of Simhabhupala, Kallinatha and Ahobala in this regard imply that nomenclature assigned to *shruti-jatis* by Bharata, is indicative of emotive power of the respective *shrutis* (vide ch. 2). Even today, the musicians attach great importance to correct intonation. Their training (*taleem*) and practice (*riyaz*) is largely aimed at refining the conception of intonation. This observation suggests that study of element of 'pitch' can lead to meaningful information about the aspect of intonation.

Although the term *shruti* invariably figures while referring to intonation in the Indian classical tradition, neither musicians nor scholars have so far agreed upon a definition of *shruti.* Therefore, during the present study, the word *shruti* is taken in a sense to describe any aspect of intonation that extends beyond the level of the gross twelve semitone categories.

As indicated in the chart, the different notes employed (content) and the manner (treatment) in which they are musically pronounced, together describe the intonation. Hence, in this study, parameter of 'pitch' is identified in order to throw light on these factors constituting intonation. Pitch is objectively measured in terms of 'frequency'. However, measuring the neuropsychological sensation of 'pitch' with the physical parameter of 'frequency' (based on number of vibrations set up in the sounding body) may not be free from limitations. Some of the studies undertaken in the area of psychology of pitch-perception have concluded that, in case of more complex tones or combinations of tones, subjective pitch may not correspond to any physically measurable frequency in the originally presented sound.[3]

Further, the totality of *raga*-structure is brought out through certain phrases that are linked to each other. In these phrases the individual notes occur with definite pitch and duration. These phrases are of two types. First, there are some catch-phrases *(pakad)* which define the core of a *raga* and secondly, there are complementary phrases that constitute the periphery of the *raga*-structure. The core phrases are among the essentials of a *raga* with almost definite structure and their presence is imperative, while the structure of the complementary phrases depends upon imagination, skill and style of the performer. Although confined by a rigid set of rules, *raga* assumes a dynamic personality in the actual performance through the core phrases as well as the complementary phrases. These phrases embody the melodic movement of a *raga*. Hence, analysis of melodic movement of the core phrases is carried out for exploring the aesthetic content of a *raga*.

Thus for the purpose of present investigation, intonation of the notes and their melodic movements have been examined. The computer set-ups used for this purpose provide a graphic representation of the melody as well as allow the pitch measurements. Considering the problems of correlating the physically measured acoustical parameter of 'frequency' representing the pitch, audibly perceived parameter of 'tonal configuration' and visually evaluated element of 'melodic shapes' (through melodic contours obtained on computer monitor) with the neuropsychologically perceived abstract feelings, the scope of this study is limited to ascertain the presence of similar intonations and melodic movements in the performance of a given *raga* by different performers. Such similitude of intonation and melodic movement, if found, can suggest a correlation between the tonal configuration of the *raga* and its aesthetic effect. Due to the various technical limitations that are involved in the working of these systems and some practical difficulties associated with the methodology, the acoustical experiments do not allow us to directly differentiate between the *rasas* of different melodies.

Alapa is one of the forms used by musicians to delineate *raga*. It is rendered at the beginning of *raga*-exposition in a very slow *(vilambit)* or medium *(madhya)* pace, with or without the drum accompaniment. Its rendition in a slow pace allows total freedom for the performer to portray the minute details of the *raga* in a leisurely manner. Regardless of the school and style of the performer, *alapa* brings forth the essence of a *raga*. Every tenet of the *raga* concerning intonation, duration and combination of notes, is observed to the last detail during the performance. Identity of the given *raga* is easy to establish during the presentation of *alapa*. The other ways of *raga* delineation like *bola, sargam, tana,* etc. may be dominated by elements such as the textual/syllabic or rhythmic content, whereas, the *alapa* section (employing vowels) due to its slow paced rendition exhibits remarkable adherence to the tonal purity. Thus, *alapa* can be undoubtedly considered to be the vital element of *raga* exposition. Hence in the present study, only *alapa* section of a performance has been considered for analysis.

In Indian tradition the human body is recognized as an instrument *(sharirivina)*. The sound produced on this *vina* is considered superior to that produced by any other instrument like *daruvivina* or the *vina* made of wood (including the flute). For the purpose of the present study, vocal music has been preferred to instrumental music on the basis of two reasons. The first being, the superior position allocated to the human voice in comparison to instrumental music. The second is the optimum efficiency achieved by the computer programs employed, for human voice. In case of Indian instrumental music, many subsidiary tones are also produced, e.g., notes given out by the auxiliary as well as the sympathetic strings of sitar. The presently available computer system processes the subsidiary sounds as well as the primary melody without any discretion, leading to confusion. Besides, the system uses a series of band-pass filters which gives meaningless display of melodic contours if faster passages involving rapid frequency changes are used. Due to these limitations, rendition of *alapa* by human voice has been preferred.

For the purpose of the present study recordings of *raga Yaman* (also known as *Kalyana*) rendered by the great singers such as late Ustad Amir Khan, Pandit Bhimsen Joshi and Dr. Prabha Atre have been selected. They are highly reputed musicians belonging to the Kirana *gharana* (school) of vocal music. Recordings of the first two musicians are taken from the archives of National Centre for the Performing Arts, Bombay (master tape nos. 1576-7 and 1235-6), while the recording of Dr. Prabha Atre has been made specially at S.N.D.T. Women's University under controlled conditions. For this recording, no drum accompaniment was allowed and the tanpura player was placed at a distance of two feet from the vocalist. The performer was requested to sing only *alapa,* preferably using syllable *aa.* In the case of first two performers' recordings no such control was possible, since these are the recordings of live performances.

The *khayal* form of *raga* exposition being currently popular in India, *alapa* component associated with the rendition of this form in vocal performance of different vocalists, has been considered suitable for analysis.

The Kirana style of vocal music is recognised as a '*svara*-oriented' style. Because of the emphasis on intonation and filigree work, this style shows preference for slow paced *alapa.* Study of intonation being the focus of the present endeavour, preference has been given to the performers belonging to this style of vocal music.

Raga Yaman, also known as *Imana* or *Kalyana,* having the Pythagorean diatonic scale is chosen for analysis. Main reason for the choice of this *raga* is the simplicity of its scale, i.e., heptatonic scale with all natural notes except the *Madhyama* or F, which is sharp. Considering the fact that the methods involved in earlier attempts to study intonation in Indian classical music were neither comprehensive nor reliable,[4] even the very basic intonational details of the natural notes need to be established and comprehended. Hence, such a *raga* has been taken for my analysis which does not employ chromatic notes. Besides, *Yaman* is a *prachalita raga* (commonly practised) in which the tonal material bears potential for unlimited melodic possibilities. Moreover, *Yaman* being one of the basic *ragas,* bears an independent and clearly distinguished aesthetic identity. Popularity of this melody among the performers, teachers as well as the listeners, has also been a matter of consideration.

Tonal material of the *raga*	Sa, Re, Ga, Ma#, Pa, Dha, Ni, or C, D, E, F#, G, A, B
Ascent	Ni, Re, Ga, Ma#, Dha, Ni, Sa'
Descent	Sa', Ni, Dha, Pa, Ma#, Ga, Re, Sa
Emphatic notes	Ga and Ni or E and B
Time	Early night
Scale type	Pythagorean diatonic

Traditional profile of *raga Yaman*

It is considered to be a rather new melody appearing on the scene of Indian *raga* system. A melody under the name *Kalyana* is first mentioned in the text of *Manasollasa* of Someshvara Deva who reigned about AD 1131. Someshvara mentions *Kalyana* or *Kalyani* as a *ragini* or a minor melody belonging to the group of *Natta-Narayana.* In the text of *Sangita Darpana* by Pandit Damodara, we find *Kalyana* described as a *raga* or major melody and given the name *Kalyana nata.* It is described as a *sampurna* or heptatonic melody using three varieties of *Rishabha.*[5] In Somanatha's *Raga Vibodha* (AD 1609), the author mentions *Kalyana* as one of the 23 *mela ragas* or parent scales.[6] The author also describes it as a *sampurna* or a heptatonic melody to be sung in the evening.

In his *Sadraga Chandrodaya,* Pundarik Vitthala (AD 1562) asserts that several melodies emanate from this heptatonic melody to be sung in the evening. However, due to the Persian influence brought about by the great poet Amir Khusro (AD 1375-1400), a new flavour was imparted to the old melody of *Kalyana* by mixing it with the imported melody of *Imana.* It is interesting to note here that the text of *Raga Tarangini* by Lochana Kavi (AD 1375-1400) asserts that the ancient masters sang twelve melodies including *Imana,* on which all the other melodies are based,[7] whereas, Pundarika Vitthala in his *raga Manjari* (AD 1600) recognizes *Yaman* as one of the 16 imported or the Persian melodies that have already obtained a place in current Indian music of North India.[8] He clearly affiliates *Yaman* with *Kalyana.*[9] The melody known as *Imana, Kalyana* or *Yaman,* is currently being practised in India.

According to the contemplative verse given in *Sangita Darpana,*[10] the visual portrait of *Kalyana* is a king carrying a sword in his hand and is valiant in warfare. According to Somanatha's *Raga Vibodha,*[11] *Kalyana* is presented in the portrait of a king. The textual and oral sources regarding *rasa* of this *raga* suggest that it has been predominantly associated with the *Shringara rasa* or the erotic mood. However, expressions such as joyful, contended, bright, active, *bhakti* etc. have also been linked with this *raga.* The findings of psycho-acoustical experiments conducted by B.C. Deva report *rasas* such as *Shringara, Vira* and *Raudra* to be associated with *raga Yaman.*[12] A *Ragamala* painting of *raga Kalyana* from Mewar school can be seen in Ill. 1 along with its poetic verse.[13]

In this study, investigations are carried out using two independent computer systems, viz. 'Melodic Movement Analyser' (MMA) and 'LVS' system.

Melodic Movement Analyser

Analysis is carried out using a Apple IIC computer set-up configured with 64K RAM, custom built interfaces viz., 'Melodic Movement Analyser' (MMA), Fundamental Pitch Extractor (FPE) and Application Software called 'MMA Software' that has been specially developed by Dr. Bernard Bel at the National Centre for the Performing Arts (NCPA), Bombay. Since no single existing machine available for the purpose of acoustic analysis can be perfectly adapted to meet the demands

Ill. 1. Ragamala Painting on Raga Kalyana

to face p. 62

of analysing a monodic music, particularly the Indian music, MMA is specially designed.[14]

Technical particulars (Hardware)

It is hardware—programmable allowing change in the hook-up of the machine's various functional blocks as well as in the output format of the digital information. The number of functional blocks of the machine is not limited and the blocks themselves are constructed as modules to fit into one or more 19-inch U.S. Standard racks. The measurement blocks described below are built to measure various specific aspects of Indian vocal and instrumental music.

It takes the output of the FPE which is close to a sine wave representing the lowest partial and connects into 16 bits

Block diagram of 'MMA 2'

Regulated Power Supply +12 +18 + 5	Frequency Generator Clock	Tape Computer Interface	Parallel Port	Blank Port	Period-meter
Block 1	Block 2	Block 3	Block 4	Block 5	Block 6

(Designed by Dr. Bernard Bel, July 1983)

Block 1 Regulated Power Supply: 230 V AC/50 Hz mains supply is rectified to provide regulated D.C. working voltages (+12, +18 & +5V) for the entire MMA blocks.

Block 2 It produces clock signals which are used by the other blocks.

Block 3 Tape Computer Interface: The block is normally situated between the output of the tape-recorder and the input of the microcomputer. This block demodulates the frequency modulated signal and the clock and synchronizing pulses are reinstated. The output of this block (logic level and clock) are directly fed into the input of a microcomputer. At present this port is not operative. It was designed for the storage of additional data such as sound energy in different bands of the spectrum, brain-wave measurements, etc.

Technical feature : 5 Volt TTL logic

Outputs : 10,000 bits/sec.

Block 4	Digital parallel inputs (Parallel Port): This block samples the information from (up to) 16 digital inputs to make it available on the single channel BUS output. Soldered straps define the value of the number of inputs validated.			
	Technical features :	TTL logic level inputs; 1 to 16 inputs per block; Output format Serial BUS output (3 state)		
Block 5	Blank for future expansion			
Block 6	Technical feature :	Format	:	16 bits
	:	Mode	:	linear periodmeter clock frequency 3.3 MHz
	:	Accuracy	:	300ns(0.01%-0.08%)

signal. Various software parameters (compression ratio, etc.) can be set from the front panels of this block.

MMA Software

The system uses a dedicated custom-designed MMA II software which is completely menu-driven. Its user-friendly interactive mode enables the researchers to 'Load' music, 'Save' the processed data, display the 'Graphic', 'Recall' data from floppy and 'Print' the graphs. It has advanced facilities like expanding and contracting the scale, zooming-in on a pre-selected area of the display and vertically shifting the basic background grid which represents a full octave range of 12 musical notes.

With the help of 'MMA', all the pitch information of a piece of music can be stored with the accuracy of digital measurements better than one cent. Use of a machine language routine, 'DATA READ' allows receiving and storing the data flow upto 10,000 bits/second while eliminating errors due to tape-speed fluctuations when the data is entered from a tape.[15] Thus a large quantity of data can be stored and processed in order to have an in-depth study of intonation.

Introduction of a 'compression' rate allows the experimenter to adjust the sampling time of (averaged) pitch measurements to suit to his requirements. Pitch measurements are 'octave shifted' so that everything fits within one octave and no period overflow is possible.[16] A specially developed logarithmic conversion technique allows the pictures derived

Ill. 2. MMA Set-up

[to face p. 65

from processing music to be displayed on the monitor screen shortly after the music has been loaded into the computer via 'MMA'.

The program 'melodic viewer' allows the computer to plot precisely the melodic lines on its screen and carry out measurements of each dot of the melodic line with a sampling time of 0.02 sec. with an accuracy better than one cent, i.e., 1/1200 of one octave.[17] Thus 'MMA' surpasses the performance of a melograph. The sampling rate may be increased from 52 (as used now) to 416 measurements per second. A faster sampling rate yields fuzzy melodic lines, whereas a slower one distorts the shapes of fast movements.[18]

Another program called 'Tonagram' evaluates the entire performance to determine the scale of the *raga* and displays the information using either linear or circular representation.

When the music is loaded into 'MMA', pitch lines appear immediately on the monitor screen with marks indicating 12 positions of equal temperament, against the background of which the pitch lines are drawn. An octave is represented in 1200 cents, thus the distance between consecutive notes is 100 cents. The dotted line represents 'Sa' (tonic). There is a 'Microscope display mode' which allows to scan a pitch line, selecting parts of it for exact analysis and measurement. Sections of pitch lines can be displayed as a sequence of numeric values and can be printed on paper. Thus MMA is indeed a microscope for music analysis. (See Ill. 2 for MMA set-up.)

LVS system

Using the 'LVS' system, the work has been carried out at the Phonetics Laboratory, University of Leiden, The Netherlands.

This system is based on the most advanced theory of pitch-perception. It uses subharmonic summation (SHS) algorithm. The SHS algorithm can be considered as a direct implementation of the concept formulated by de Boer (1977) that subharmonics are actually generated in the central processor.[19]

The SHS model assumes that each spectral component activates not only those elements of the central pitch processor that are most sensitive to the frequency of this component but also those elements that have a lower harmonic relation with this component. The contributions of the various components add up and the activation is highest for that frequency—sensitive element that is most activated by its harmonics, which is the fundamental.[20] Thus SHS tries to mimic the pitch processor in the auditory central nervous system. This algorithm provides a way to calculate the fundamental frequency that best fits the harmonic structure of the spectrum[21] and hence can be presented as a fine model representing a biological system where nonlinearities are essentially used to increase the versatility of the system.[22] 'LVS' (PDT 1200) using SHS algorithm is an adaptation made by J. Pacilly for musical analysis and has one cent precision.[23]

The program 'Pitch Plotter' written by Wim van der Meer in Microsoft Quick Basic 1.0 enables to examine the files created by LVS on VAX. Pitch Plotter is by and large a MacIntosh implementation of the 'Melodic Movement Analyser' (MMA) software developed by Bernard Bel for the Apple II series. The size of the 'Pitch Plotter' file is limited to 10,000 points (100 points = 1 sec., i.e., 100 seconds or 20 screens). The standard screen shows 5 seconds of the file. By clicking and dragging the mouse over a pitch line, any portion of the melody can be analyzed. The program offers various menus such as File, Edit, Window, Analysis, Sound and Settings with several sub-options.[24] Further details of the 'LVS' system along with functional aspects of the 'Pitch Plotter' program are given later in this chapter.

Methods adopted for acoustical analysis of *raga-rasa*

Procedures involved in processing and analysing the data on the 'Melodic Movement Analyser' and 'LVS' system are different.

Method for working with 'Melodic Movement Analyser' (MMA)

The complete experimental hardware set-up configures Apple IIC 64K RAM computer system with the custom-built interfaces like Fundamental Pitch Extractor (FPE), Melodic Movement Analyser II (MMA II) and a Graphic Equaliser. The block diagram of the set-up is as follows:

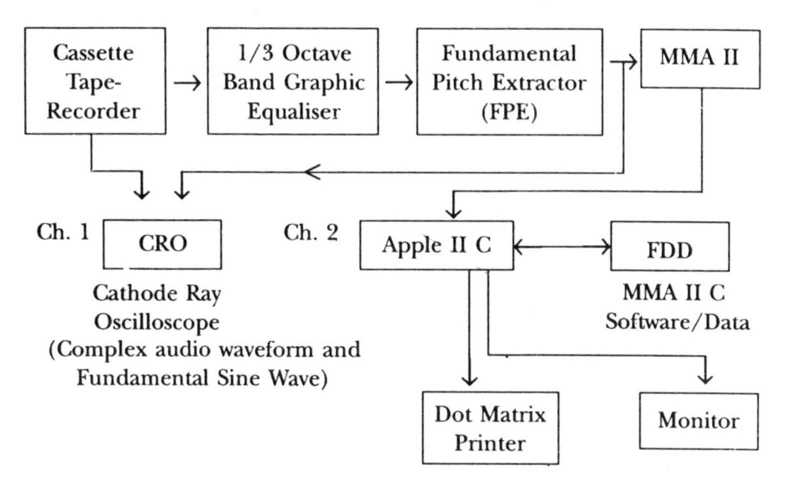

The set-up also indicates inclusion of a cassette tape-recorder for feeding the music data and a cathode ray oscilloscope for simultaneous display of waveforms corresponding to the output of tape-recorder (complex audio waveform) and the filtered signal (Fundamental Sine Wave) going into 'MMA'.

Cassette Tape-Recorder: Music is transferred from the spools (Master Tapes) to cassette tapes. Using a low frequency generator and a frequency counter, the frequency of the key-note given out by tanpura (an instrument providing the continuous drone which is tuned to the key-note of the musician) is measured and entered so that the computer can store its average value. This key-note frequency for Amir Khan (AM) is 140.3 Hz.,for Bhimsen Joshi (BJ) it is 140.4 Hz. while for Prabha Atre (PA) it is 210 Hz. These are the averages of several individual values obtained over many days. These measurements are repeated many times to avoid any error due to subjectivity in the pitch-perception.

Graphic Equaliser: The frequency of the fundamental (key) note thus measured, helps to adjust the filters of Graphic Equaliser (1/3 octave band). These filters are manually adjusted to band-limit the audio spectrum around the aurally-judged frequency of the fundamental note. The adjustment of filters of the Graphic Equaliser brings about filtering of harmonics in a coarse manner.

Fundamental Pitch Extractor: In the Fundamental Pitch Extractor (FPE), fine filter adjustment is made and thereafter the pitch extraction takes place automatically. The FPE uses a series of sixteen 4th order bandpass filters (Q=9) covering the range 60 Hz. to 2000 Hz. in 1/3 octave steps. The FPE assumes that the lowest frequency periodical signal whose energy represents a given fraction of the total sound energy, is the fundamental. The outputs of the sixteen 1/3 octave bandpass filters are rectified. A counter activated by a 1000 Hz. clock scans the output of sixteen rectifiers in order to determine which one is tracing the fundamental. A reference voltage is determined by dividing the peak amplitude of the input signal by a given number. As soon as one of the DC outputs is found to be greater than the reference voltage, the FPE assumes that the corresponding bandpass filter is capturing the fundamental. Consequently, the current value of the counter is latched in a memory and a 16-to-1 line multiplexer connects the output of the filter to the output of the FPE. This action can be visualised on the front panel—one of the 16 LEDs will be lighted indicating which filter has been selected.

The output of the FPE is then fed to the periodmeter of MMA, which gives a digital output related to the frequency of the fundamental. The extracted analogue fundamental signal is seen in the form of a pure sine wave on CRO. This waveform can be compared with the simultaneous display of waveform corresponding to the complex signal coming out of the tape-recorder to ensure filtering of harmonics.

MMA: The digitised signal is formatted (data, sync, clock) to feed into the computer serial port. It is stored in the computer memory (RAM) in the form of 'Melodic Files', so that any section of music can be recalled on the monitor. In addition, the same digital data is stored on external floppy disk for enabling repeated recall and to study in future.

With the help of an additional tape-recorder the musical data being processed is acoustically stored on the tape, so that it could be precisely related to the graphic output of the computer. The pitch-lines appearing on the monitor screen are refined to remove glitches that appear each time the pitch extractor switches from one bandpass filter to the next.[25] Then the entire pitch-line corresponding to the section of the performance being analysed is printed out using a Dot Matrix Printer.

After having the melograms (graphic representation of the melody) on paper, detailed transcription is attempted by repeatedly listening to the relevant section of the melody. This process is so laborious that, to transcribe a piece of melody of 10 seconds duration, 15 to 20 minutes of concentrated efforts are involved. However, the process of transcription has its own advantages. By correlating the graphic contours with the acoustical information, minute details of the melodic progression can be studied. Attack, sustain and decay stages of the individual notes in varied contexts are also examined.

Observations have been made regarding the influence of different vowels and consonants employed by the singers, upon the pitch-line. Complex characteristics of various embellishments employed by the singers, such as the *andolan, murki, gamaka, kan,* etc., can be comprehended from the graphic details. Further, melodic phrases are analysed with a view to understand the manner in which the tones are linked to form a phrase. Interesting observations have been made by comparing the graphs of the same phrase intoned by different singers or by the same singer at different stages of performance. Certain characteristic features associated with the singer's style have also been studied. In addition, the study of graphic details has allowed to comment upon the variance in the manner of intonation in the ascending and descending movement of notes.

Using the mode of 'minitonagram', pitch measurements are made only for the standing notes of atleast 0.5 second duration. The term 'standing note' implies a note that is audibly perceived as a 'steady note' or that which is judged as a *khada-sura* by the north Indian musicians. The pitch measurements are obtained in 'cents'. A range of an octave is represented by 1200 cents. Expression of intonation in cents should be taken as a statistical indication and interpretation of its significance needs proper contextual considerations. The criteria of measuring a steady note has been evolved after having comprehended the difficulty associated with accurately measuring 'the ideal pitch' of a note of shorter duration, linked by ascending or descending melodic contexts. In Indian music, glides and undulations are so common that only 10-20% of even the *alapa* section of a performance consists of so-called 'steady notes' or the sustained notes. Graphs 1 and 2 represent 'minitonagram' showing display of the tonal distribution of a selected section of a melogram. In this mode, scale of representation is enlarged considerably using the program 'microscope'. From each enlargement a 'tonagram' is made which is referred to as a 'minitonagram'. The peak in the figure indicates the average frequency of the note under consideration.

For a given performer, average value of intonation for each occurrence of the given steady note is measured and then averaged out to arrive at a single average value in cents for that note. Earlier on, the pilot study conducted for *raga Bhimpalasi* has revealed that pitch measurements for the notes intoned with *gamaka, meend,* etc., show wide range or deviation.[26] The melodic contours of these intonations seem to be musically more significant than their pitch information. Hence, pitch measurements for such intonations have not

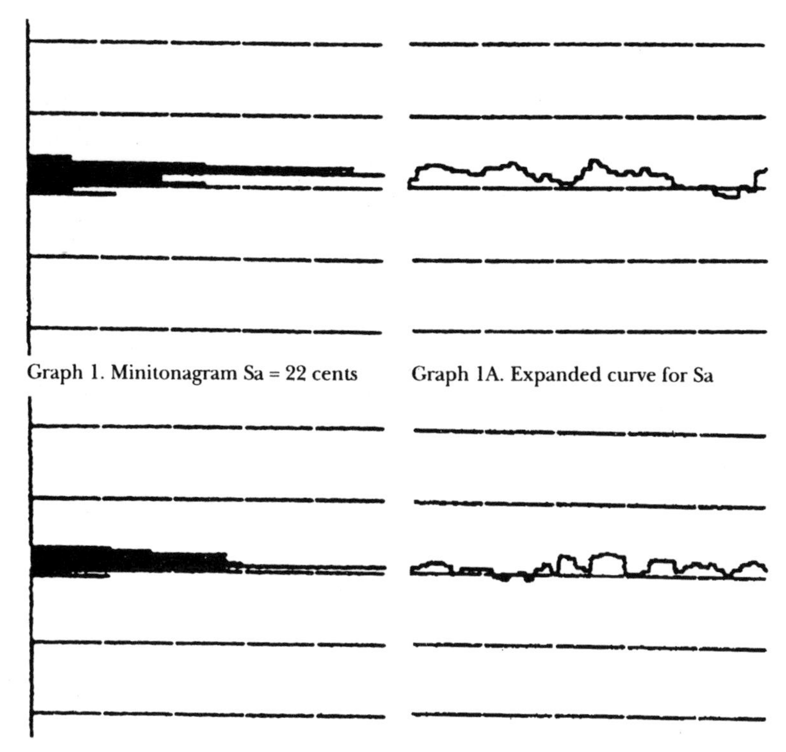

Graph 1. Minitonagram Sa = 22 cents

Graph 1A. Expanded curve for Sa

Graph 2. Minitonagram Sa = 11 cents

Graph 2A. Expanded curve for Sa

been attempted, instead their melodic shapes are studied.*

Method for working with 'LVS' system

This process involves creating melodic files of musical data with 'LVS' system on 'VAX' computer first and then processing them on MacIntosh using 'Pitch Plotter' program. This system relies heavily on the powerful computers which require very little manual effort. Melodic files of maximum length 60 seconds are created using the same recordings (i.e. *Yaman* rendered by PA, BJ and AM). Using the Pitch Plotter program, these files can be viewed. The standard screen shows 5 seconds of the file. By clicking and dragging the mouse over a pitch-line, that portion can be analyzed.

*The expression 'melodic shape' implies pitch in time and does not refer to the form of objects in space.

Among the various options that are available in the 'menu', 'analysis' offers two sub-options viz., 'tonagram' and 'selective'. The 'tonagram' gives a plain histogram of all the points plotted in the file. It first comes up with a visual image, followed by the numerical statistics. 'Selective' is also a kind of 'tonagram', but it only looks at tones that satisfy a number of conditions. These conditions are set with the 'PARAMS' item including the frame size (in hundredths of a second) and the permitted standard deviation. Thus the information obtained by 'analysis' are average frequency (arithmetic average within the range of each note), standard deviation (the average standard deviation of a note) and weight (the number of times a note with the length set in 'PARAMS' occurs). The visual representation of stability of the note, i.e. weight/standard deviation is also given.

Graph 3 shows graphic representation of melody on LVS and graph 4 displays selective tonagram obtained on LVS. In this system, option of using sound is available which is useful for verifying the correct movement, especially after editing a melodic line or by using interpolation.

Graph 5 represents graphic contour of a melody obtained on MMA and graph 6 shows its edited version.

For each performer, the pitch data obtained from 'MMA' and 'LVS' analysis are tabulated against the theoretically expected values. From the frequency values corresponding to the individual notes, measurements corresponding to the intervals between the consecutive notes and those having 'fifth' relation are calculated. The adjacent intervals and 'fifths' in addition to the measurements against the reference of Sa, are calculated to avoid errors that might arise from the instability of the reference tone i.e. Sa, which can get shifted by few cents during the course of the performance and the performer may use the new reference to intone the subsequent tones. In such cases, the subsequent intonations may be judged as 'out of tune', if the 'fifth' are not measured.*

*For more details, refer to the case of shehnai performance reported by Bel, (ISTAR, project # 1), in *ISTAR Newsletter* 2, p. 56.

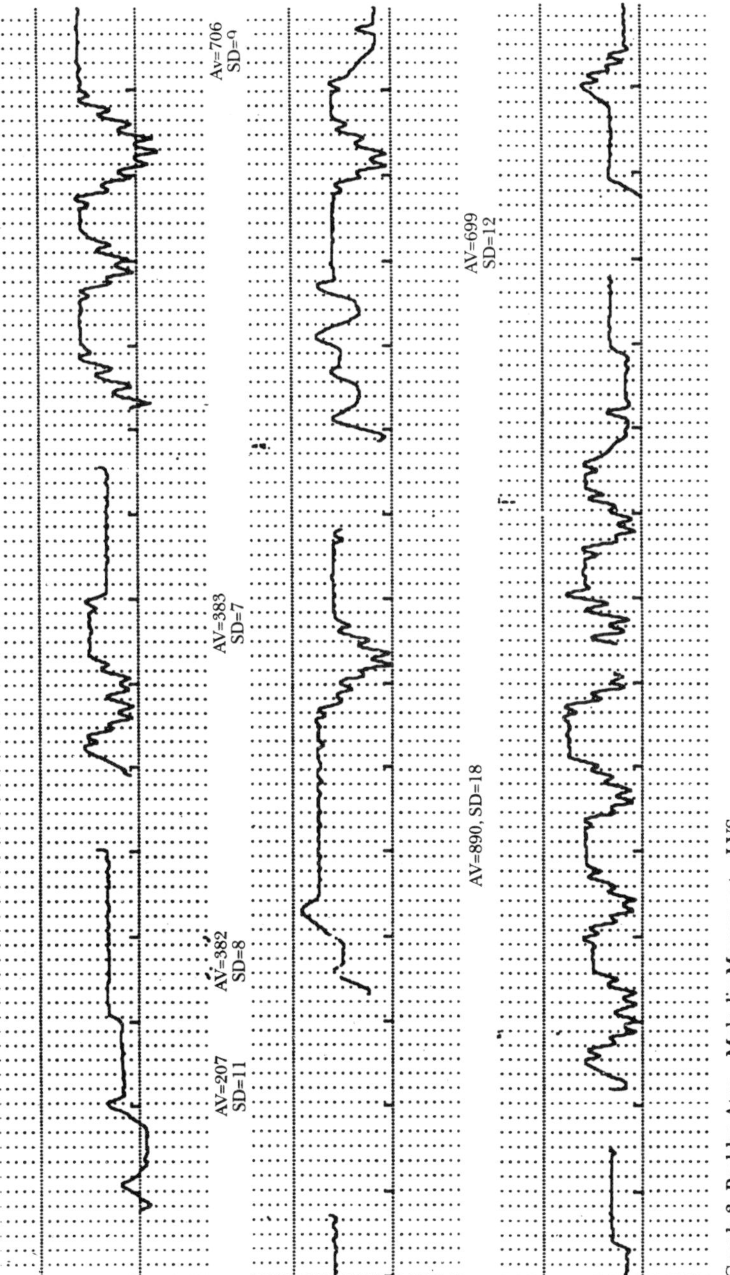

Graph 3. Prabha Atre—Melodic Movement—LVS

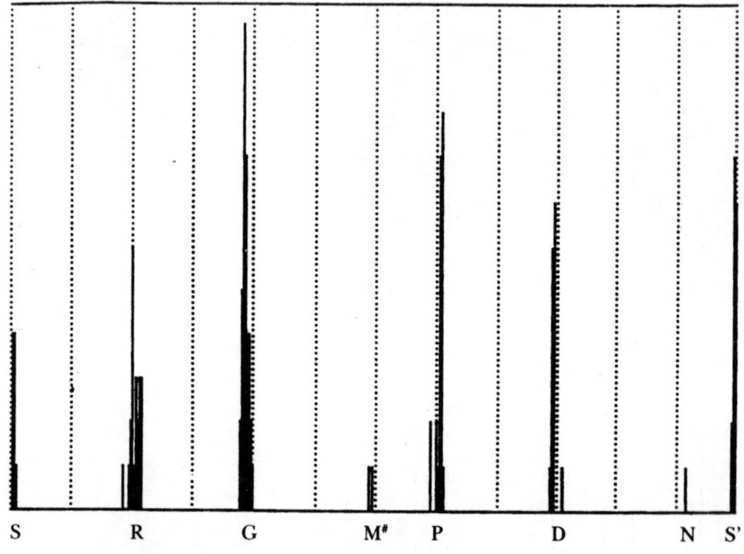

Graph 4. Tonagram—LVS

Step = 12 frame = 50 MAX SD = 25 MAX Angle = 20

svara	*cents*	*weight*	*SM*
R	204	264	3
G	385	444	2
M	590	24	2
P	703	276	2
D	892	180	1
N	1114	12	0
S	1199	312	2

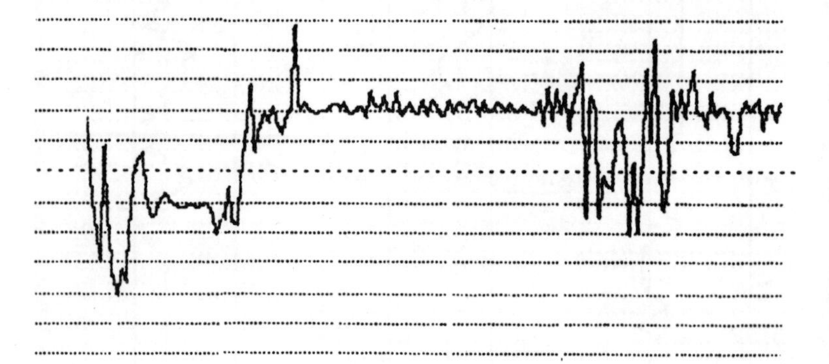

Graph 5. Graphic contours with glitches

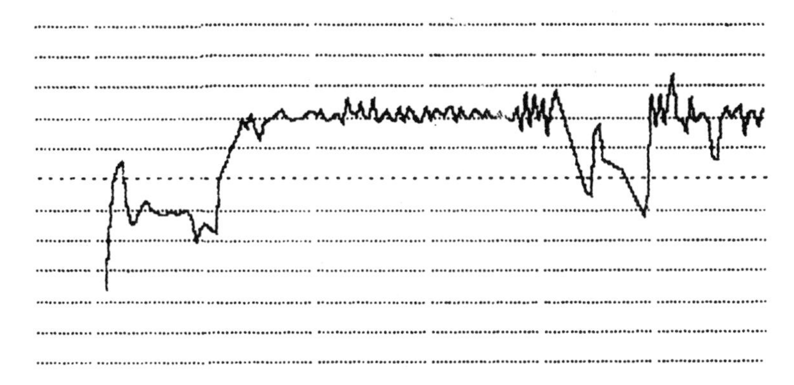

Graph 6. Edited contour

The comparison of the pitch data experimentally obtained using the two independent systems with the theoretically calculated values, has allowed to comment upon the pitch values (corresponding to different tones) conceptualised by the individual performer for the given *raga*. The pitch data obtained for all the three performers when compared, allowed to assess the coherence as well as variance in pitch values assumed for different notes by these performers for the given *raga*.

The pitch data that has been experimentally obtained during the course of present study is also compared with the pitch data obtained by van der Meer et al.[27] on 'MMA' for the same *raga Yaman*. This additional data was available for Bhimsen Joshi, Mallikarjuna Mansur and Malini Rajurkar. The methods adopted for measuring pitch during the investigation carried out by van der Meer et al. are different.

Theoretically, the notes comprising the scale of *raga Yaman* and *Marubihaga* are the same.* Hence the pitch-measurements obtained by van der Meer et al.[28] for *raga Marubihaga* rendered by PA and BJ are compared with those obtained for *raga*

*Strictly speaking, the note *Shuddha madhyama* which is sparingly used in *Marubihaga*, does not figure in *raga Yaman* at all. The variety of *Yaman* that employs this note is called *Yaman-Kalyana*. Barring this difference, the notes used in *Yaman* and *Marubihaga* are the same.

Yaman rendered by the same performers during the present investigation.

The examination of pitch lines obtained for the entire performances of PA, BJ and AM has permitted to make observations pertaining to the melodic movement of the *raga Yaman*, as it was expounded by each of these three vocalists. During this process, the melodic graphs are continuously compared with the relevant sections of the actual melody. Factors like; stages through which the *raga* has been expounded, the melodic centres used, the manner in which each of these centres has been developed, certain common note combinations, different melodic strategies adopted by the performers to create aesthetic atmosphere, etc., are considered to comprehend the complete progression of the *raga* in case of these three performers.

Thus in the present study, pitch data is experimentally obtained using 'MMA' and 'LVS' system, whereas the melodic lines obtained from 'MMA' are analysed to understand the various nuances of melodic progression with respect to *raga Yaman.*

References

1. Arthur Jacob, *The New Penguin Dictionary of Music,* p. 277.
2. R.K. Shringy and Premlata Sharma, trs., op. cit., vol. I, p. 407.
3. R. Plomp, *Aspects of Tone Sensation: A Psychological Study,* pp. 112-14; W. Ward, in *Journal of Acoustical Society of America,* pp. 369-80.
4. Bernard Bel, in *ISTAR Newsletter* 2, pp. 7-12.
5. *Sangita Darpana,* Saraswati Mahal Series, no. 34, v. 271.
6. *Raga Vibodha,* R. Aiyar's edn., p. 58.
7. *Raga Tarangini,* p. 3.
8. O.C. Gangoly, *Raga-s and Ragini-s,* p. 56.
9. O.C. Gangoly, in *Sangeet Natak,* p. 13.
10. *Sangita Darpana,* v. 37, p. 47.
11. *Raga Vibodha,* v. 200, p. 77.
12. B.C. Deva, *The Music of India: A Scientific Study,* p. 184.
13. Klaus Ebeling, *Ragamala Painting,* p. 131.
14. Bel and Arnold, in *NCPA Quarterly Journal* XII, 2-3, p. 46.
15. Ibid., p. 49.

16. Ibid.
17. Bernard Bel, in *ISTAR Newsletter* 3-4, pp. 54-59.
18. Ibid.
19. Dik Hermes, in *Journal of Acoustical Society of America* 83 (1), p. 262.
20. Ibid., p. 258.
21. Ibid., p. 262.
22. Ibid., p. 263.
23. Wim van der Meer, Personal Communication, 1990.
24. Ibid.
25. Bernard Bel, in *ISTAR Newsletter* 3-4, pp. 54-59.
26. Suvarnalata Rao et al., in *Journal of Acoustical Society of India,* vol. XVII (3 & 4), pp. 273-76.
27. Wim van der Meer, Personal Communication, 1990.
28. Ibid.

Chapter 5

Results Accrued from the Experiments

In this chapter the results obtained from the analysis of performance of *raga Yaman* by Amir Khan (AM), Bhimsen Joshi (BJ) and Prabha Atre (PA); are presented along with the discussion. The data regarding the pitch measurements (using two systems viz., 'MMA' and 'LVS'), observations pertaining to different vocal inflections and those related to the melodic movement that is characteristic of the *raga* being rendered (*Yaman*); are presented separately.

Pitch measurements for individual notes

Pitch measurements carried out by employing the technique of 'minitonagram' on 'MMA' for the three performances viz., AM, BJ and PA for *raga Yaman* (as described in chapter 5) are presented in Table 16.

The comparison of the pitch values corresponding to different notes intoned by three different musicians while performing the same *raga* indicates that the pitch values corresponding to Sa, obtained for PA, BJ and AM are nearly equal.* However in case of AM, values corresponding to all the other notes are consistently lower as compared to those for PA and BJ.

*A difference of few cents in the pitch measurement can be due to various factors such as the wow or flutter introduced by the sound recording and reproducing machines as well as due to the tonal influence of accompanying musical instruments and syllables. Hence during the interpretation of the pitch data a maximum difference of ± 10 cents is overlooked. Intonation within this range is considered to be consistent.

TABLE 16
Pitch Measurements on 'MMA' for 'PA', 'BJ'&'AM'

Note		*Average pitch value in cents*		
Western	*Indian*	*Amir Khan*	*Bhimsen Joshi*	*Prabha Atre*
C	Sa	4	–2	4
		(10)*	(31)	(11)
D	Re	195	198	201
		(10)	(9)	(11)
E	Ga	389	397	395
		(28)	(13)	(12)
F#	Ma#	585	594	616
		(12)	(7)	(6)
G	Pa	687	700	708
		(18)	(22)	(6)
A	Dha	—	904	900
			(4)	(4)
B	Ni	1089	1102	1109
		(5)	(4)	(4)

*The figures in the parentheses represent the number of occurrences of a given note for which the average pitch measurements are calculated.

There appears to be a good consistency among all the three performers regarding the intonation of Re and Ga. Average values for the Ga for *raga Yaman* as reported by other researchers are 408 cents, 392 cents[1] and 404 cents.[2] However, the differences in the methodology involved do not allow to compare these results with the results reported here. Considerable difference in frequency is observed regarding the intonation of Pa and Ni. No measurement could be obtained for Dha intoned by Amir Khan. Although there have been a few occurrences of this note with enough duration, the graphic contours representing this note are invariably fuzzy and hence no measurement could be attempted. Thus, no comments can be made regarding the pitch of this note. It is interesting to observe that except for Ma#, all the other pitch values obtained for PA and BJ, are in close agreement and these values are slightly but significantly highter than those obtained for AM.

These results indicate that there is a good agreement regarding the intonation of six out of seven notes studied, in case of two out of the three performers. A considerable variation in the pitch values corresponding to certain notes intoned by different singers might be due to the tonal influence of accompanying instruments like tabla, tanpura, harmonium and/or the different syllables used to intone the notes. This is not to suggest that these factors (except the syllables) influence the actual intonation of the singer, but due to the technical limitations of the analyzing system to discriminate between the main voice and the accompanying instruments (which follow with almost same pitch). These factors bring about variation in the graphic lines that are presumed to represent these notes. Besides, the accompanying syllables cannot be possibly separated from the tone and hence the tonal influence due to them will be seen in the pitch values as well as in the melodic contours of the notes. This aspect is discussed in more detail in the latter part of this chapter.

Besides the pitch values corresponding to individual notes, values corresponding to the intervals of adjacent notes and the 'fifths' are also calculated. Table 17 shows these values for all the three performers.

The Table 17 indicates that in case of all the three performers, the intervals of Sa-Re and Re-Ga are matching. In case of AM and BJ, there is a good agreement for the intervals of Ga-Ma# and Ma#-Pa. However, PA's intonation of Ma# and Pa being sharper than the other two performers (see Table 16), values for the same intervals are either higher or lower. Similarly, AM's intonation of Ni being lower than the other performers, the interval Ni-Sa in his case is considerably augmented as compared to that in case of BJ and PA.

Although there are significant differences in the pitch values corresponding to certain notes intoned by all these performers, the average values corresponding to the 'fifths' (Sa-Pa, Pa-Re, etc.) in case of each performer are in close agreement. The average value for all the 'fifths' as shown in Table 17 for AM, BJ and PA works out to be 693 cents, 699

TABLE 17
Interval-Comparison

Interval	*Average pitch value in cents*		
	Amir Khan	*Bhimsen Joshi*	*Prabha Atre*
Sa-Re	191	200	197
Re-Ga	194	199	194
Ga-Ma#	196	197	221
Ma#-Pa	102	106	92
Pa-Dha	—	204	192
Dha-Ni	—	198	209
Ni-Sa	111	100	95
Sa-Pa	683	700	708
Pa-Re	708	698	693
Re-Dha	—	706	699
Dha-Ga	—	693	695
Ga-Ni	700	705	724
Ni-Ma#	696	692	707

cents and 704 cents respectively. Each figure is arrived at by averaging out the values of all the 'fifths' for a given performer.

The examination of the pitch values corresponding to adjacent intervals for a given performer (individually) indicates that every singer has maintained almost equal interval between Sa-Re, Re-Ga, Ga-Ma#, Pa-Dha and Dha-Ni (exception PA for Ga-Ma#). Similarly, all of them are consistent as far as values for intervals of Ma#-Pa and Ni-Sa are concerned. Thus, internal agreement (i.e. comparing different intervals of a given performer) between one semitone intervals (like Ma#-Pa or Ni-Sa), two semitone intervals (like Sa-Re, Re-Ga and others) and the 'fifths', indicates that when compared with others, a given performer may show difference in pitch value for a given note, however when considered individually, every performer seems to be balancing the intonation of individual notes, so as to maintain consistent intervals.

The pitch measurements are also carried out using another independent system, viz. 'LVS'. Table 18 presents the measurements corresponding to individual notes, adjacent intervals and 'fifths' in case of all the three performers.

TABLE 18
'LVS' Measurements

Notes/Interval	*Average pitch value in cents*		
	Amir Khan	*Bhimsen Joshi*	*Prabha Atre*
Sa	0	–7	–1
Re	199	200	204
Ga	384	394	391
Ma#	589	590	613
Pa	678	692	702
Dha	910	—	891
Ni	1087	1096	1115
Sa-Re	199	207	205
Re-Ga	185	194	187
Ga-Ma#	205	196	222
Ma#-Pa	89	102	89
Pa-Dha	232	—	189
Dha-Ni	177	—	224
Ni-Sa	113	111	86
Sa-Pa	67	699	702
Pa-Re	721	708	703
Re-Dha	711	—	687
Dha-Ga	674	—	700
Ga-Ni	703	702	724
Ni-Ma#	702	694	698

No measurements could be obtained for Dha using this system, for BJ. Comparison of the pitch values of different notes and intervals reveals that there is a good consistency of intonation for the notes Sa, Re, Ga and note-intervals Sa-Re, Re-Ga for all the three performers.

Observations regarding the adjacent intervals of individual performer (no inter-comparison) indicates that all the two semitone intervals like Sa-Re, Re-Ga, etc., are in close agreement for BJ, whereas, in case of AM, Re-Ga and Dha-Ni are slightly lower while Pa-Dha is quite high. The intervals of Re-Ga and Pa-Dha were found to be in close agreement in case of PA.

The one semitone intervals such as Ma#-Pa and Ni-Sa are matching in case of BJ and PA, whereas, value of Ma#-Pa interval for AM is lower due to low intonation of the note Pa.

As in the case of Table 17 showing 'MMA'-values for different intervals, this Table also shows that the average value of 'fifths' in case of each of the performer is 698 cents, 700 cents and 702 cents respectively. This indicates that among different performers, slight variations may occur with respect to the pitch of adjacent tones, but the intonations of larger intervals (such as fifths) are balanced so as to maintain the intervals consistent.

The pitch measurements obtained for each of the performers using 'MMA' and 'LVS' are separately tabulated with the theoretically expected values of the corresponding notes and intervals. The formula used for arriving at a theoretical value in cents is given as: 1200 times the logarithm on the base 2 of the frequency ratio. By this formula, the interval of 3/2 (frequency ratio between Sa-Pa) will be $= 1200 \times \log_2 (3/2) = 701.955$ cents = 702 cents. Using this formula intervals between different notes can be theoretically calculated. Table 19 shows comparison of pitch values for Amir Khan.

This Table indicates that pitch values assumed for the notes Ma#, Pa and Ni are lower than the expected values. Hence intervals like Ga-Ma#, Sa-Pa, Ga-Ni etc. are affected. However, the measurements obtained with MMA and LVS show a good agreement (except for Pa-Re). Even though the pitch of Ni and Ma# is lower than the expected values, the interval Ni-Ma# is in agreement with the expected value.

Table 20 shows comparison of pitch values for Bhimsen Joshi. The values for Ga are slightly higher than the expected values, whereas, those for Ma# and Ni are significantly lower. Hence, the intervals like Ga-Ma# and Ma#-Pa, Dha-Ga and Ga-Ni seem to be affected. Even though the values for both, Ma# and Ni are lower than expected, the interval of Ni-Ma# is consistent with the expected value. A close agreement between 'MMA' and 'LVS' values can be noticed in case of BJ. In addition, the intervals of Sa-Pa, Pa-Re and Re-Dha are matching with the expected values.

Table 21 indicates that the value for Dha (on LVS) is lower

TABLE 19
MMA-LVS Comparison for Amir Khan

Notes/Interval	*Average pitch value in cents*		
	MMA	*LVS*	*Expected*
Sa	4	0	0
Re	195	199	204
Ga	389	384	386
Ma#	585	589	612
Pa	687	678	702
Dha	—	910	906
Ni	1089	1087	1110
Sa-Re	191	199	204
Re-Ga	194	185	182
Ga-Ma#	196	205	226
Ma#-Pa	102	89	90
Pa-Dha	—	232	204
Dha-Ni	—	171	204
Ni-Sa	111	113	90
Sa-Pa	683	678	702
Pa-Re	708	721	702
Re-Dha	—	711	702
Dha-Ga	—	674	680
Ga-Ni	700	703	724
Ni-Ma#	696	702	702

than the expected value, hence the intervals of Re-Ga and Dha-Ni are augmented. However, all the 'fifths' are matching with the expected values except for Dha-Ga and Re-Dha (for LVS only). As in case of AM and BJ, the pitch values obtained on MMA and LVS show good matching, thus showing reliability of the measurements.

As described in chapter 4, the pitch data collected by van der Meer et al. for *raga Yaman* on MMA for BJ, Mallikarjuna Mansoor (MM) and Malini Rajurkar (MR) was procured. Table 22 shows comparison of pitch values obtained for BJ by van der Meer et al., using 'tonagram' on MMA with those obtained during the present study by using 'minitonagram' on MMA. The latter method though manual, allows to relate the intonation to the melodic context and specific note treatment.

TABLE 20
MMA-LVS Comparison for Bhimsen Joshi

Note/Interval	*Average value in cents*		
	MMA	*LVS*	*Expected*
Sa	–2	–7	0
Re	198	200	204
Ga	397	394	386
Ma#	594	590	612
Pa	700	692	702
Dha	904	—	906
Ni	1102	1096	1110
Sa-Re	200	207	204
Re-Ga	199	194	182
Ga-Ma#	197	196	226
Ma#-Pa	106	102	90
Pa-Dha	204	—	204
Dha-Ni	198	—	204
Ni-Sa	100	111	90
Sa-Pa	700	699	702
Pa-Re	698	708	702
Re-Dha	706	—	702
Dha-Ga	693	—	680
Ga-Ni	705	702	724
Ni-Ma#	692	694	702

Table 22 shows that the pitch measurements for all the notes using two different methods seem to be in agreement. Considering the fact that in the 'tonagram' method a pitch window allowing a small deviation is specified so that the computer can scan such notes, it is evident that with such specification the computer selects only the standing notes of specified deviation. Thus, it is not surprising that the two methods provide almost the same results. Further, this may suggest that the manual method of 'minitonagram' involving labour and time could be well replaced by the 'tonagram' method. However, bearing in mind the disadvantage of losing the critical element of 'context', technique of 'minitonagram' should be preferred.

TABLE 21

MMA-LVS Comparison for Prabha Atre

Note/Interval	*Average value in cents*		
	MMA	*LVS*	*Expected*
Sa	4	–1	0
Re	201	204	204
Ga	395	391	386
Ma#	616	613	612
Pa	708	702	702
Dha	900	891	906
Ni	1109	1115	1110
Sa-Re	197	205	204
Re-Ga	194	187	182
Ga-Ma#	221	222	226
Ma#-Pa	92	89	90
Pa-Dha	192	189	204
Dha-Ni	209	224	204
Ni-Sa	95	86	90
Sa-Pa	708	702	702
Pa-Re	693	703	702
Re-Dha	699	687	702
Dha-Ga	695	700	680
Ga-Ni	724	724	724
Ni-Ma#	707	698	702

TABLE 22

BJ—Two independent measurements

Note	*Average value in cents*	
	Tonagram (in cents)	*Minitonagram (in cents)*
Sa	–4	–2
Re	209	198
Ga	392	397
Ma#	599	594
Pa	706	700
Dha	899	904
Ni	1104	1102

Comparison of the pitch data obtained in this study for AM, BJ and PA with the data obtained by van der Meer et al.

TABLE 23
Measurements for different performers in cents

Note	*Amir Khan*	*Bhimsen Joshi*	*Prabha Atre*	*M. Mansoor*	*M. Rajurkar*	*Expected*
Sa	4	−2	4	4	4	0
Re	195	198	201	204	204	204
Ga	389	397	395	396	396	386
Ma#	585	594	616	614	614	612
Pa	687	700	708	709	709	702
Dha	—	904	900	904	904	906
Ni	1080	1102	1109	1094	1094	1110

for the same *raga* by MM and MR is presented in Table 23.

This Table reveals that there is a general agreement in the intonation of all the notes except Ma#, which is lower than expected in case of AM and BJ. However, as pointed out earlier, both these performers have also intoned Ni with slightly lower pitch; thus balancing the 'fifth' interval.

A significant shift in the values of the notes Ma#, Pa, Dha, and Ni is often due to a particular tanpura tuning. In case of 'Pa Sa Sa Sa' tuning, two references viz., Pa and Sa are available for the singer. These reference points being located at the beginning and in the middle of the scale, lend appropriate guidance for intonation of any note in the scale. Whereas, in case of 'Ni Sa Sa Sa' tuning, which is also very popular (even when the *raga* allows the use of *Panchama*) among the singers; both the reference points being in the extreme positions, intonation of notes from Pa onwards may get affected.

Pitch data obtained for *raga Yaman* during the present study was compared with the data obtained by van der Meer et al. for *raga Marubihaga;* for PA and BJ. The Table 24 presents the information regarding the pitch-values obtained for individual notes in these two *ragas* for PA and BJ.

Table 24 representing the data regarding pitch values of the same notes occurring in two different *ragas* indicates that no significant difference is observed in the values corresponding to a given note, except for Re and Pa in case of BJ.

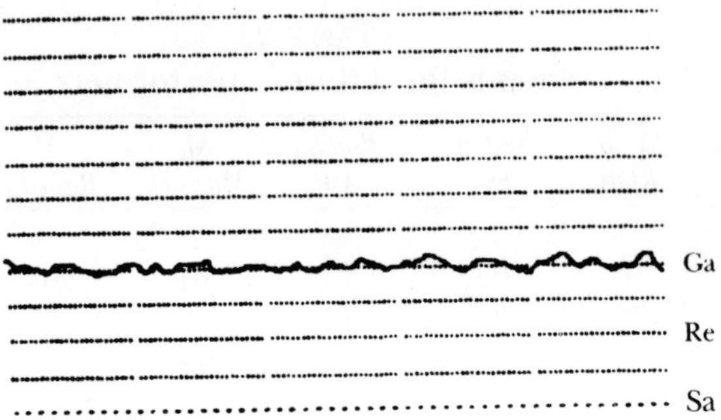

Ga
Re
Sa

Graph 7. Amir Khan—Ga

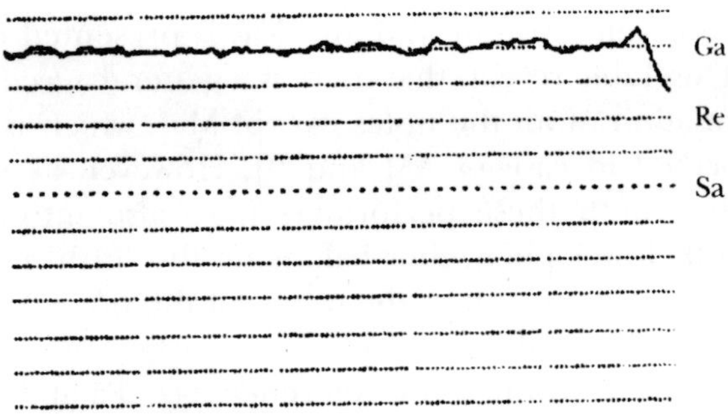

Ga
Re
Sa

Graph 8. Amir Khan—Ga

Sa
Ṇi

Graph 9. Prabha Atre—Ṇi

TABLE 24
Yaman-Marubihaga comparison

Note	*Average value in cents*			
	Prabha Atre		*Bhimsen Joshi*	
	Yaman	*Marubihaga*	*Yaman*	*Marubihaga*
Sa	4	12	–2	7
Re	201	206	198	220
Ga	395	403	397	400
Ma#	616	606	594	604
Pa	708	702	700	712
Dha	900	902	904	902
Ni	1109	1116	1102	1102

In *Marubihaga,* both these notes are intoned sharper as compared to their intonation in *Yaman,* by BJ.

The melodic progression of all the notes in these two *ragas* is quite different, e.g. in *Marubihaga* Re and Dha occur only in the descending passages while in *Yaman,* both these notes are invariably present in the ascending movement. A given note occurs with definite preceding and succeeding notes in a given phrase and thereby exhibits a tonal influence of these notes. The differences observed with respect to the pitch of certain notes could be attributed to this tonal influence. Even though for pitch measurements only the 'steady' part of a note isolated from its transient and decay is considered, the influence due to these stages is noticed in the 'steady' section of the note. On the other hand, a good agreement observed in case of majority of the notes suggests that the tonal ranges assumed by the notes in these two *ragas* are not very different.

Details of vocal inflections

Comparison of the pitch-lines obtained for the entire performance of these three performers leads to certain general observations regarding vocal inflections. In the following graphs, the horizontal lines indicate semitones

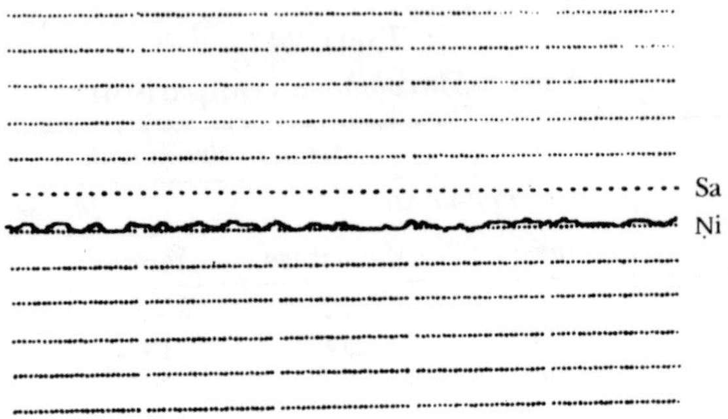

Sa
Ṇi

Graph 10. Prabha Atre—Ṇi

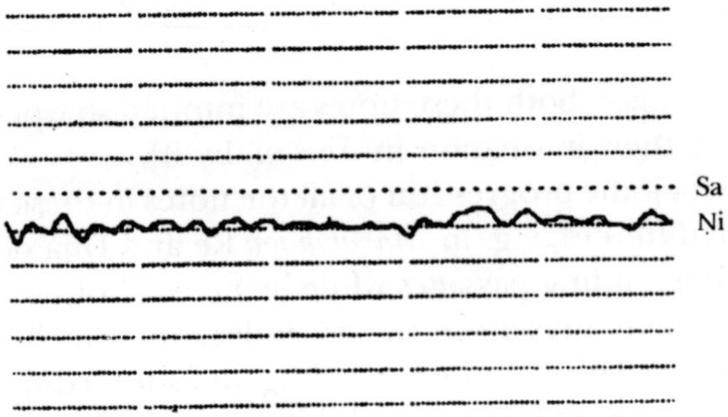

Sa
Ṇi

Graph 11. Bhimsen Joshi—Ṇi

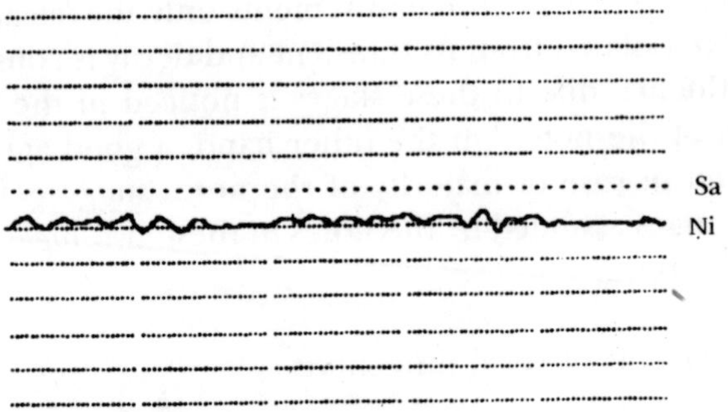

Sa
Ṇi

Graph 12. Bhimsen Joshi—Ṇi

(100-cent steps). The horizontal (time) scale is identical in all graphs and the dotted line indicates Sa or C. Every note is represented by the first letter of the Indian name, e.g., *Shadja*—S, *Rishabha*—R and so on. A note in lower case indicates shorter duration than that represented in upper case. A note appearing in superscript indicates *kan*. The sign such as / or \ before a given note indicates attack from the lower and higher pitch position respectively. Information with *meend* (glide) is shown as \ or/.

(a) *Steady notes*

Graphs 7 to 12 represent melodic lines corresponding to steady tones of duration of at least 0.5 sec. The expression 'steady' implies a tone aurally judged to be non-varying with respect to pitch; by the trained musicians. These intonations are accompanied by various preceding and following melodic contexts which may not be seen on the sections of graphs presented here. Graphs 7 and 8 show Ga being intoned as a steady note by Amir Khan. In the first instance the frequency is 403 cents, while in the second intonation it is 411 cents. The first Ga is embedded in the ascending line preceded by Re, while the second Ga is a part of a descending melody and is attacked from Ma$^{\#}$.

Graphs 9 and 10 show intonation of steady Ni by Prabha Atre. The first graph representing Ni which is preceded by a brisk murki involving Re and Sa, has a pitch value 1113 cents. Whereas, the second Ni is intoned as a concluding part of a melodic phrase involving ascending movement, i.e. Ga Ma$^{\#}$ Dha-Ni and has the pitch of 1105 cents in the beginning, slowly rising up to 1119 cents and finally decreasing to 1106 cents before fading out with of 1103 cents.

Graphs 11 and 12 show steady Ni intoned by Bhimsen Joshi. In graph 11, a direct attack on the desired note is observed. The initial frequency is 1092 cents which rises steadily to 1102 cents first and then rises further up to 1110 cents indicating larger deviation towards the decay stage. The graph 12 represents melodic line corresponding to Ni,

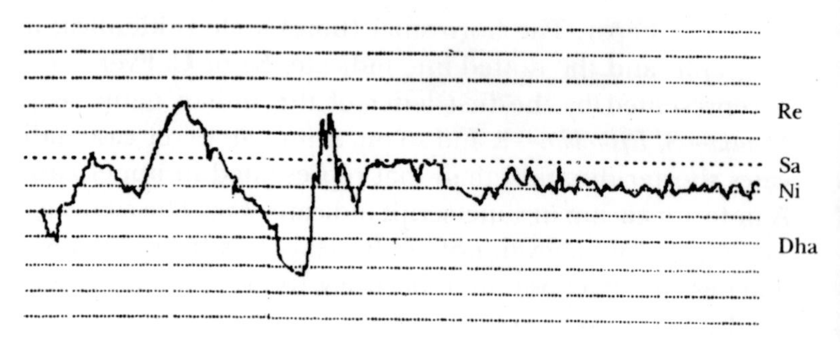

Graph 13. Amir Khan—Ḍ^{s}ṆRḌ^{r}SṆ

which is intoned after Dha, i.e., ṆḌṆ. A smooth transition from Dha to Ni is noticed. The attack shows frequency of 1102 cents which gradually decreases to 1097 cents. Thus, it can be seen that the preceding and the following contexts are the decisive factors that govern the melodic contour and subsequently the tonal range assumed by the steady notes.

(b) *Ascent and descent*

Graphs 13 to 15 show melodic lines corresponding to ascending and descending lines. Graph 13 represents Amir Khan's rendering of a phrase 'Ḍ^{s}ṆRḌ^{r}SṆ'. The desired transition from Dha to Ni is via Sa. Again, the progression from Dha to Sa at the end is with a touch of Re, before arriving at Sa.

Similar tendency of an indirect attack can be seen in graph 14 showing intonation of 'G$^{M\#}$G^{P}M$^{\#P}$M$^{\#}$D\G$^{m\#}$P' by Prabha Atre. The smooth unbroken melodic line indicates the entire execution being achieved in a single breath. A uniform rounded approach for all the notes before approaching the final Pa, is evident. At some instances, the indirect approach is due to an attached grace note or *kan* which is clearly audible. However, at many instances these 'via-modes' elude the aural perception, although a definite rounded movement is identified by a trained ear.

Graph 15 represents Bhimsen Joshi's intonation of 'RṆḌ Ṃ$^{\#}$Ḍ^{s}Ṇ R^{n}R′'. In this example also, the rounded approach for

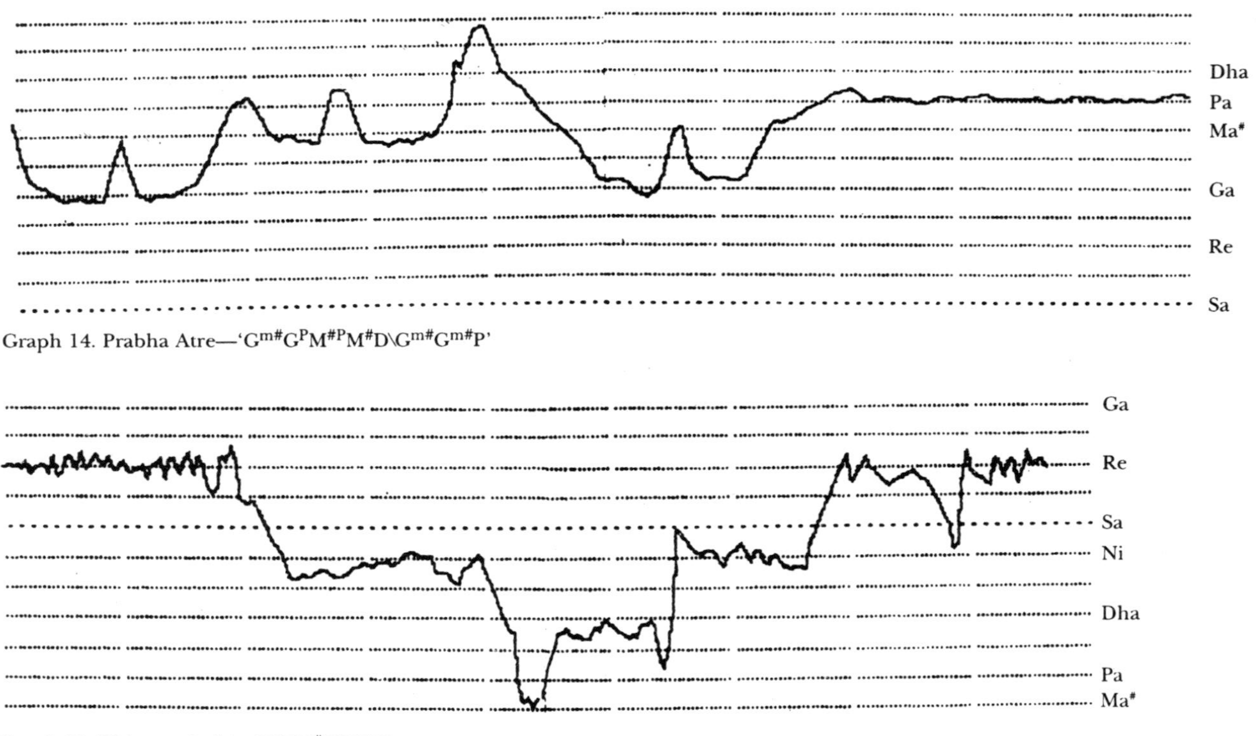

Graph 14. Prabha Atre—'$G^{m\#}G^{P}M^{\#P}M^{\#}D\backslash G^{m\#}G^{m\#}P$'

Graph 15. Bhimsen Joshi—$R\underset{.}{N}\underset{.}{D}\underset{.}{M}^{\#}\underset{.}{D}^{s}\underset{.}{N}R^{n}R$

certain notes is clearly noticed. Further, analysis of several segments involving either ascent or descent or both these movements, reveals that the speed of rendering and duration of individual notes influence the contours of the embedded notes. When a given phrase is rendered in a considerably lower speed, direct attack on the desired note is rarely observed. It is often associated with undershooting or overshooting of the pitch before attaining the desired position. Whereas, the same phrase rendered with increased speed leads to decreased duration for individual notes and their progression, especially in the descending movement where it is observed to be far more direct.

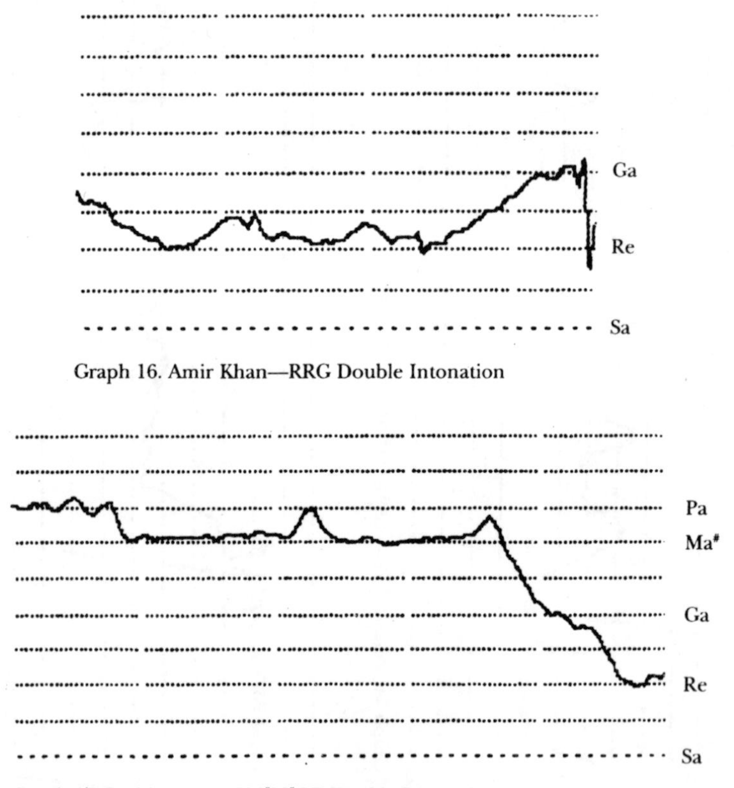

Graph 16. Amir Khan—RRG Double Intonation

Graph 17. Prabha Atre—PM#M#GR Double Intonation

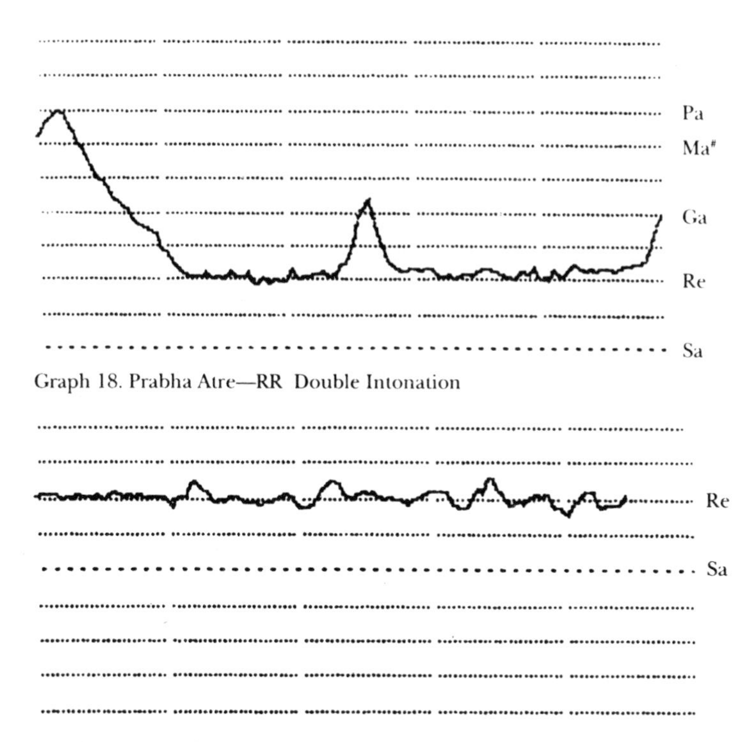

Graph 18. Prabha Atre—RR Double Intonation

Graph 19. Amir Khan held Re with *andolan*

(c) *Double intonation*

It is observed that a special technique is employed by the singers to lend an aesthetic effect to a given note. This technique involves holding the note steady for a small duration and then attacking the note again with a touch *(kan)* of an adjacent note. Such intonation with respect to Re by AM indicated in graph 16 shows that the initially pronounced note was immediately followed by its recurrence. In this case, the re-attack on the desired note is made from an augmented pitch-position. Graph 17 indicates intonation of Ma# by PA. After having held the initially pronounced Ma# for a small duration, the note is again attacked using a touch of higher note, i.e., Pa. Graph 18 shows the same tendency of holding Re with a touch of Ga, by PA. Repeated intonation of a given note probably allows a momentary modification in the vocal

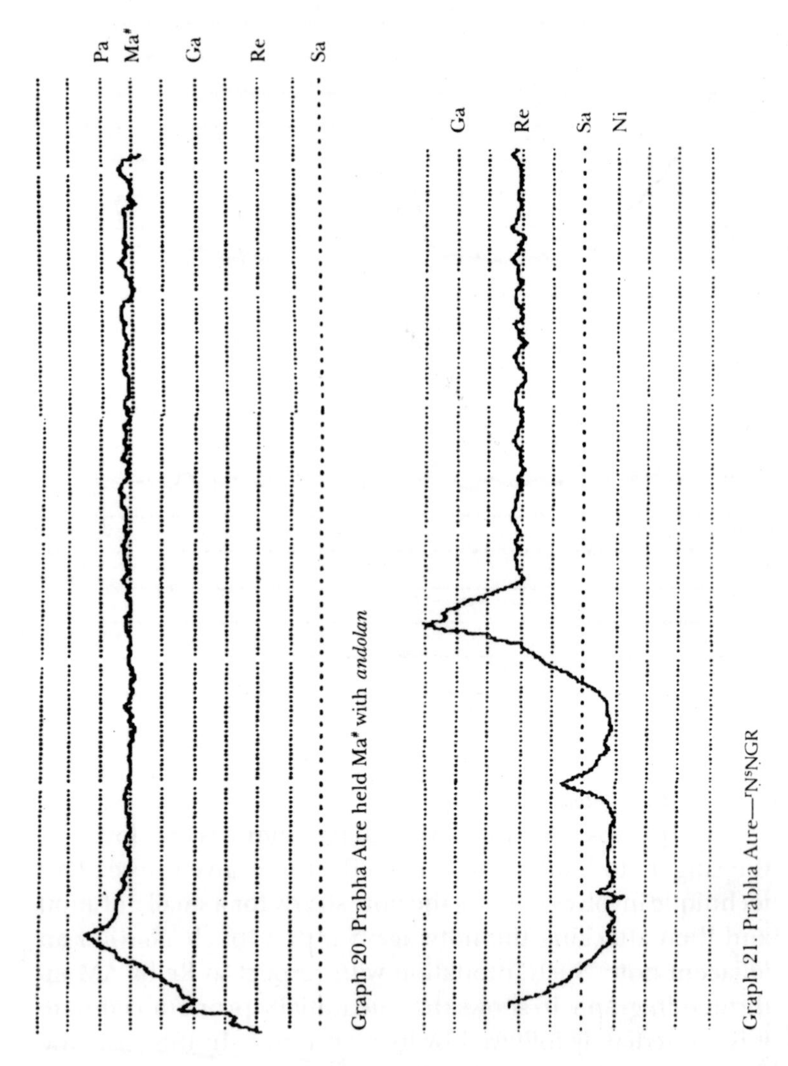

Graph 20. Prabha Atre held Ma* with *andolan*

Graph 21. Prabha Atre—^{r}Ṇ^{s}ṆGR

tract and thereby serves as an aesthetic means for facilitating the sustenance of a note.

(d) *Note held with andolan*

A subtle technique employed to fade out a steady note has been observed. The decay of the steady note is achieved by using *andolan* which is a vibratory movement executed

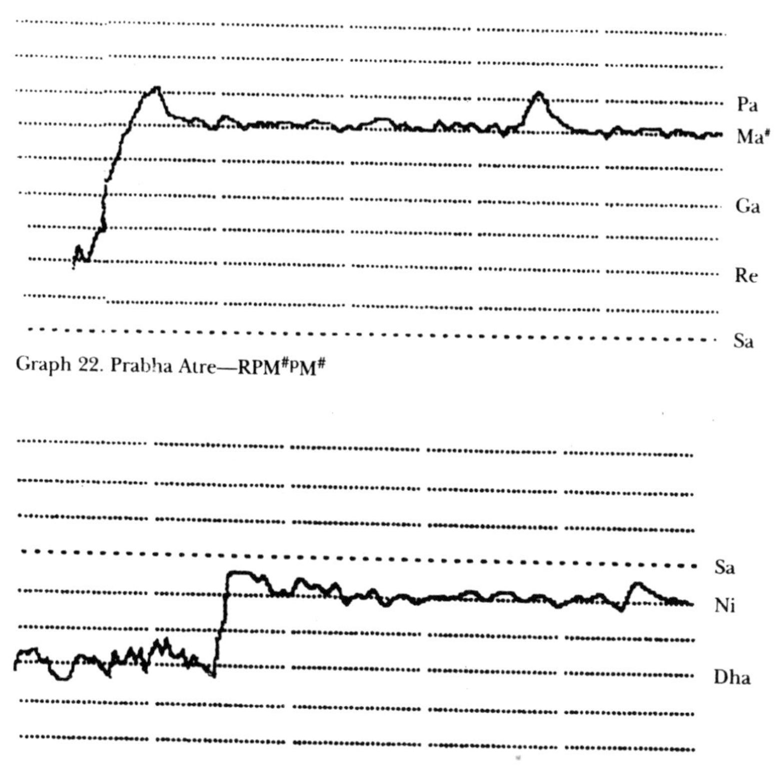

Graph 22. Prabha Atre—RPM$^{\#}$PM$^{\#}$

Graph 23. Bhimsen Joshi—Ḍ^{s}Ṇ

under perfect control, resulting into small but regular deviations from the reference tone. In some *ragas,* the use *andolan* for particular notes is highly characteristic, e.g., Ga in Darbari or Re and Dha in Bhairava. However, these intonations are quite different in terms of pitch variations and in their aesthetic significance as compared to the ones being discussed here. Besides lending an aesthetic effect to the steady note, this technique seems to involve less physical efforts than those required for steady sustenance of a note. Intonation of Re ending in *andolan* by AM is shown in graph 19 and a similar intonation of Ma$^{\#}$ by PA can be seen in graph 20.

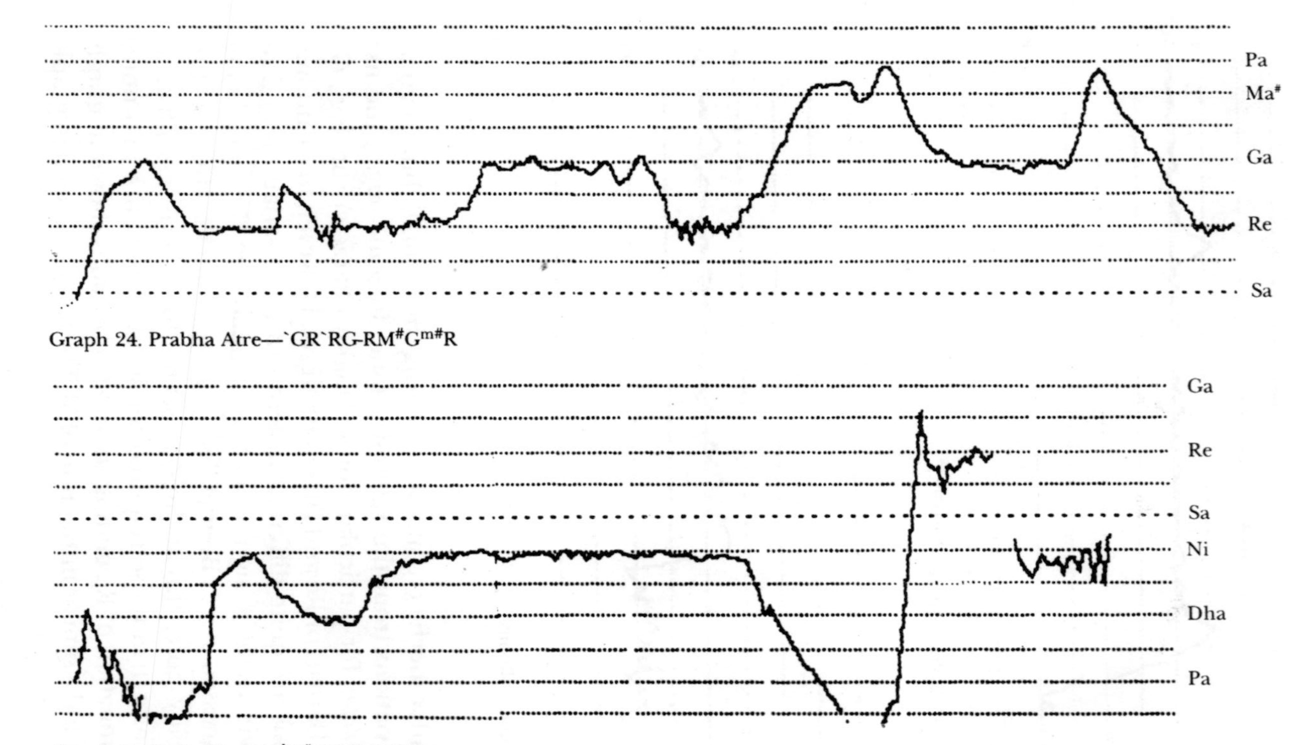

Graph 24. Prabha Atre—`GR`RG-RM$^{\#}$G$^{m\#}$R

Graph 25. Amir Khan—^{d}M$^{\#n}$DNDPM$^{\#}$RN

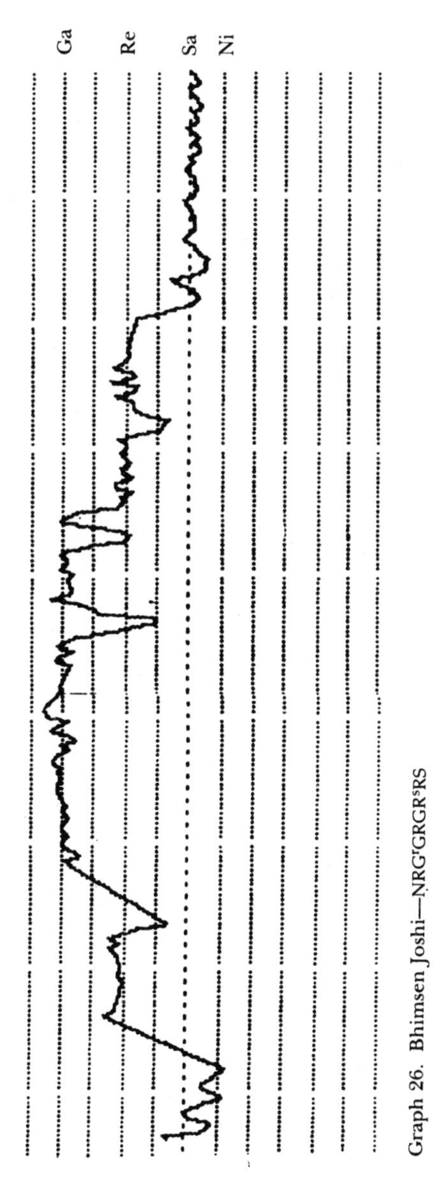

Graph 26. Bhimsen Joshi—ṆRG^{r}GRGR^{s}RS

(e) *Intonation with kan*

The word *kan* indicates a slight touch or grace of another note used for intoning a given note. Most of the time, these graces can be audibly perceived by a trained ear. However, sometimes it can elude aural perception. In such cases, transcription and such melodic graphs prove extremely useful. Graph 21 represents intonation of phrase ^{r}Ṇ^{s}ṆGR by PA. The melodic contours indicate *kan* of Re for the initial Ni and that of Sa for the second Ni. Similarly, graph 22 shows rendering of Ma$^{\#}$ with a *kan* of Pa intoned by PA. Similar *kan* of Sa for Ni can be observed in graph 23 showing rendering of a short phrase ḌṆ, by BJ.

(f) *Intonation with meend*

It is an embellishment commonly used by the musicians to enable a smooth gliding transition between the notes. A phrase GRRGRM$^{\#}$G$^{m\#}$R lasting for about 1.5 sec., intoned by PA is represented in graph 24. An unbroken melodic contour implies a single-breath execution of the phrase. Besides a smooth progression from one note to the other, the graphic contour also reveals a presence of subtle *kans* or graces. Distinct touch of Ni and Ga for the initial Re, support of Ga for the second Re and *kan* of Ma$^{\#}$ for the last Re is clearly observed. Graph 25 represents a continuous phrase ^{d}Ṃ$^{\#n}$ḌṆḌṖṂ$^{\#}$ṚṆ intoned by AM. Similar to graph 24, this melodic line also represents subtle *kans* embedded in the smooth gliding execution. Another continuous phrase intoned by BJ is shown in graph 26. The phrase is ṆRG^{r}GRGR^{s}RS involving rapid movements of the notes towards the end.

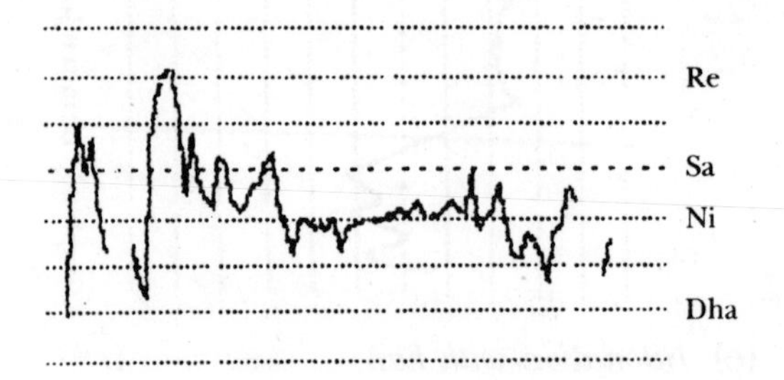

Graph 27. Amir Khan—ṆRSSṆ

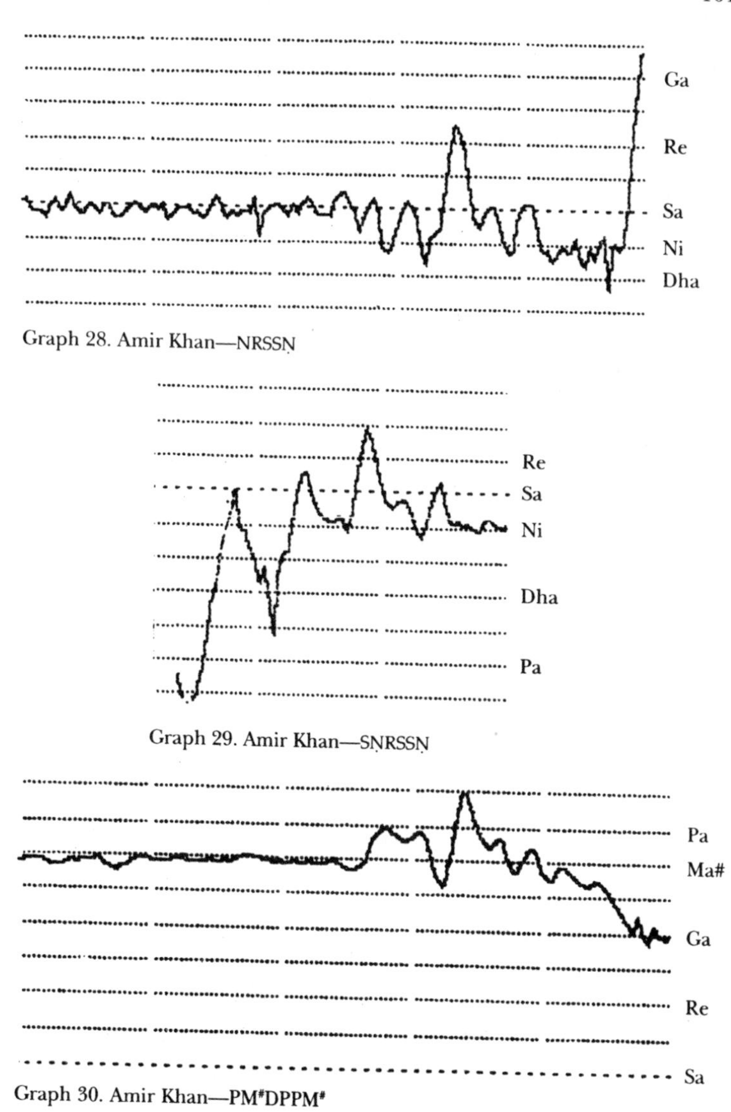

Graph 28. Amir Khan—NRSSṆ

Graph 29. Amir Khan—SṆRSSṆ

Graph 30. Amir Khan—PM#DPPM#

(g) *Intonation with murki*

It is an embellishment involving brisk movements of notes. The graphs 27 and 28 represent a phrase ṆRSSṆ intoned by AM using *murki*. The graph 29 represents a phrase SṆRSṆ, while graph 30 indicates a very similar intonation of

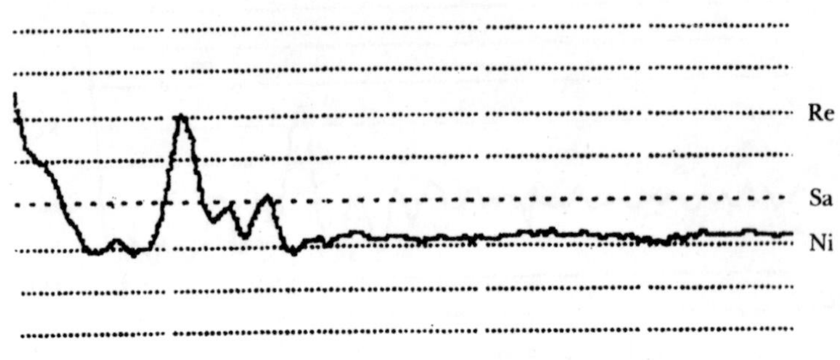

Graph 31. Prabha Atre—NRṢSṆ

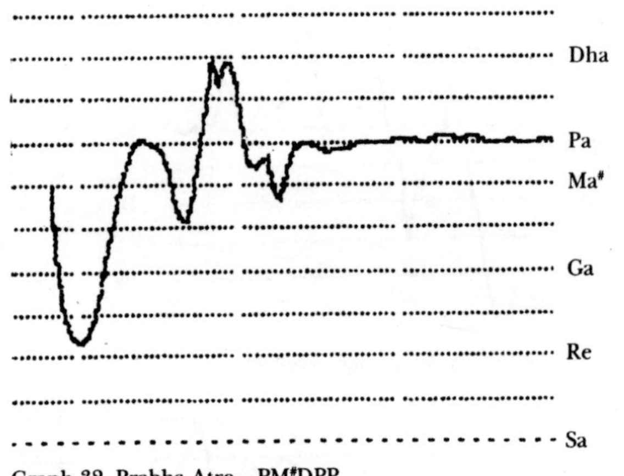

Graph 32. Prabha Atre—PM#DPP

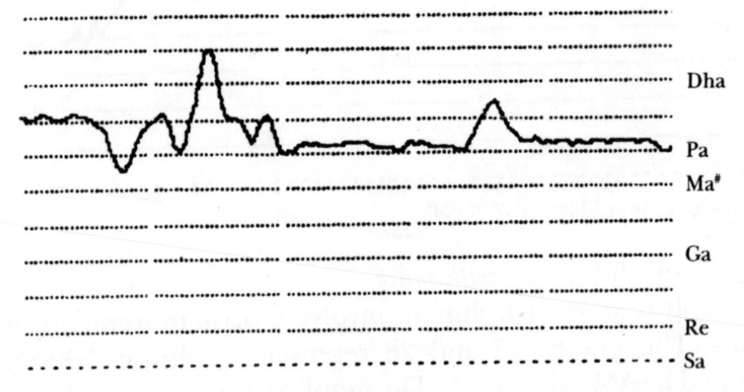

Graph 33. Prabha Atre—M#PM#DPPM#

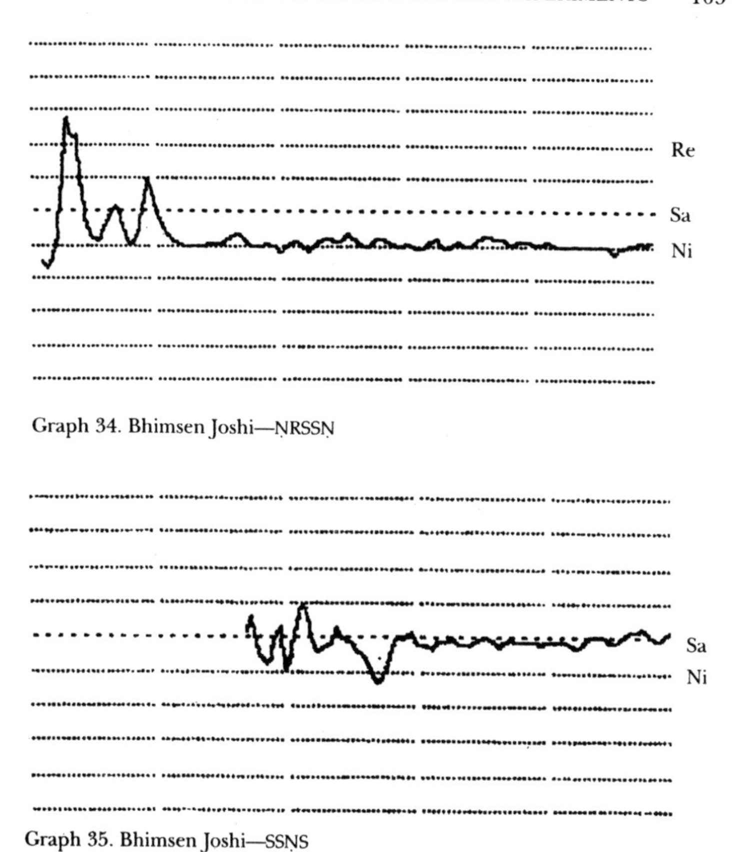

Graph 34. Bhimsen Joshi—ṆRSSṆ

Graph 35. Bhimsen Joshi—SSṆS

PM$^{\#}$DPPM$^{\#}$ by the same performer. A phrase ṆRSSṆ intoned using the same technique by PA can be seen in graph 31, whereas, similar renderings of PM$^{\#}$DPP and M$^{\#P}$M$^{\#}$DPPM$^{\#}$ by PA are indicated in graphs 32 and 33. Likewise, graph 34 shows BJ's intonation of ṆRSSṆ. The graph 35 represents phrase SSṆS rendered with combination of *khatka* and *kan.* The details of the physical characteristics appear to be far more intriguing as compared to their audibly perceived tonal structure. At number of instances, various notes involved in a *khatka* and *murki* seem to shift from their normally expected pitch positions. However, a good deal of coherence can be observed in the melodic contours of similar phrases intoned

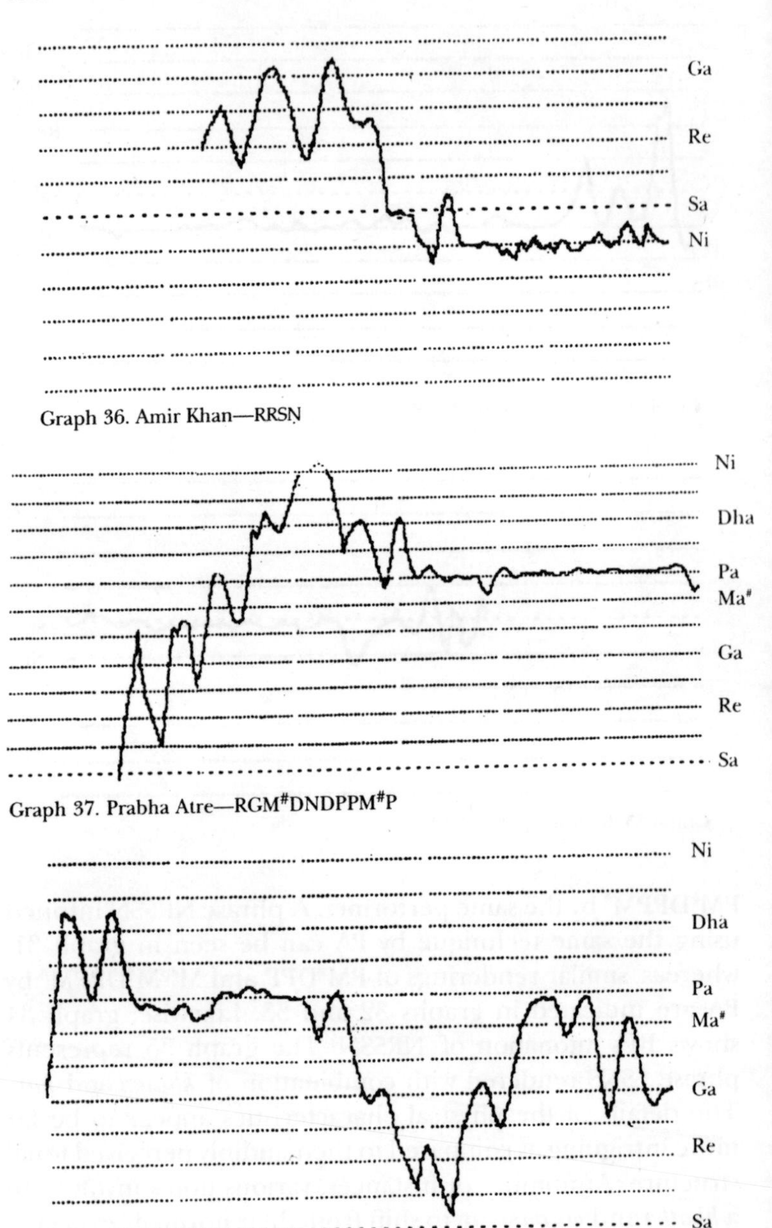

Graph 36. Amir Khan—RRSṆ

Graph 37. Prabha Atre—RGM#DNDPPM#P

Graph 38. Prabha Atre—GDPPM#GRRGPM#GG

using the above technique by different performers. The complexities of speed and intonation of notes associated with *murki* and other embellishments, seem to cause variation in the pitch value. The inherently complex nature of these embellishments make the pitch measurements impossible. All the same, in a given context, the acceptability of these altered pitch values at the perceptible level, and also their aesthetic relevance, is indeed noteworthy.

(h) *Intonation with gamaka*

An ornamental feature involving oscillatory movement ranging between tonal space of two notes, is identified as *gamaka*. Graph 36 shows expansive *gamaka* movements occur-

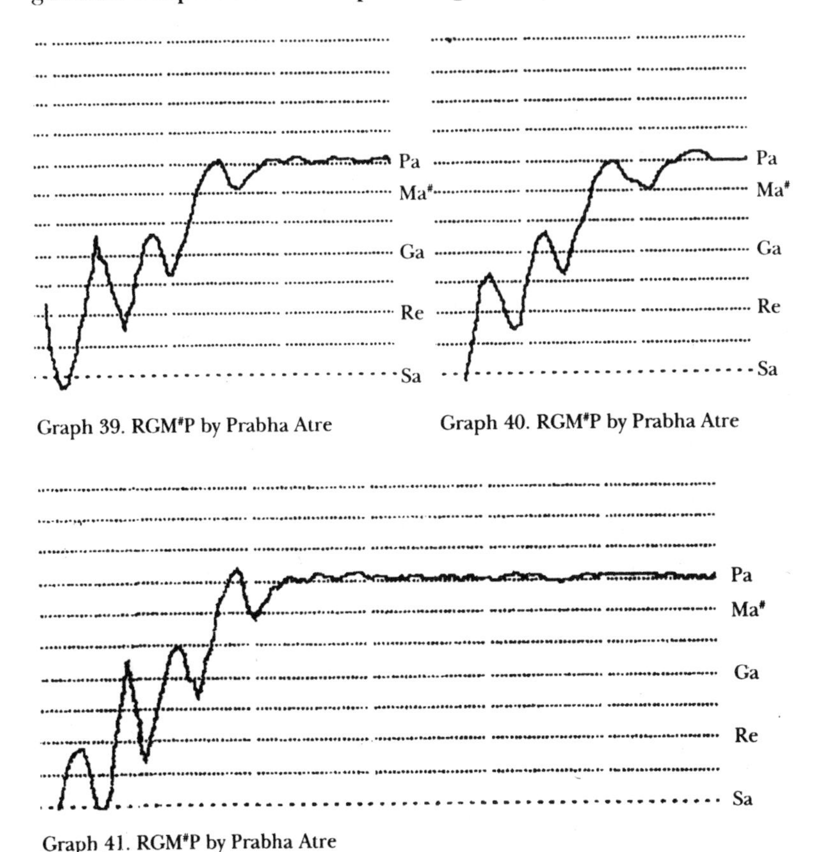

Graph 39. RGM$^{\#}$P by Prabha Atre

Graph 40. RGM$^{\#}$P by Prabha Atre

Graph 41. RGM$^{\#}$P by Prabha Atre

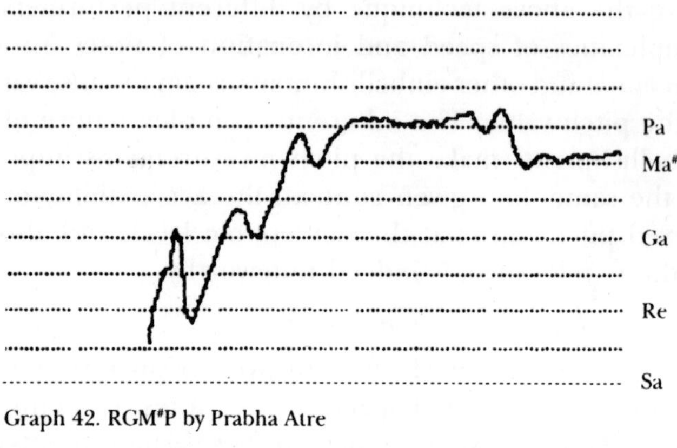

Graph 42. RGM#P by Prabha Atre

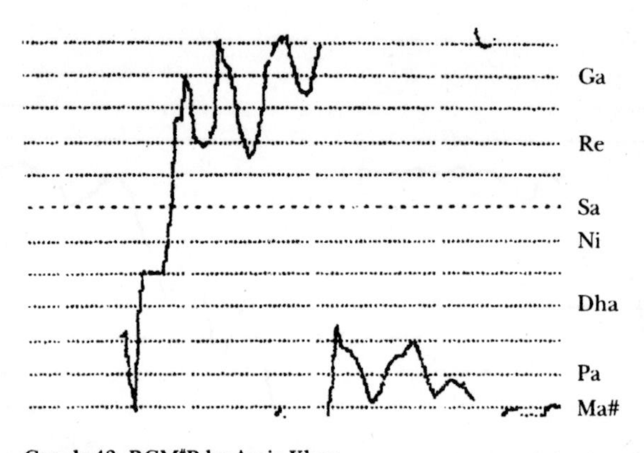

Graph 43. RGM#P by Amir Khan

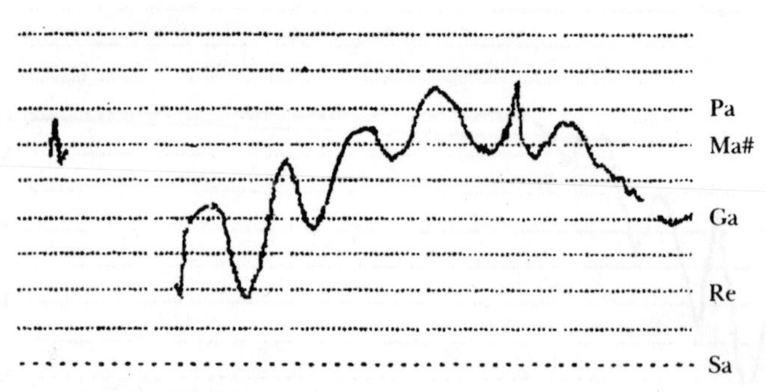

Graph 44. RGM#P by Amir Khan

ring within the tonal space between Re and Ga. The Graphs 37 and 38 represent intonation of a phrase with *gamaka,* by PA. In the first graph, the initial segment of RGM# as well as Pa in the later half of the phrase is intoned with *gamaka.* In Graph 38, the oscillatory Pa seems to occupy the tonal space from Pa to Dha. Similarly the oscillatory Re occurs within the tonal space of Sa and Re. All the illustrations provided here suggest that, during the *gamaka* movements entire tonal space between a given note and its adjacent note is explored.

(i) *Same phrase intoned at different instances*

Graphs 39 and 40 show rendering of a phrase RGM#P by PA in a slow manner. Graphs 41 and 42 show the same phrase being rendered in faster tempo by the same performer. Comparing the first phrase with the second and the third phrase with the fourth, we observe that the melodic contours

INTONATION OF GA WITH VOWEL/CONSONANT (GRAPHS 45-51)

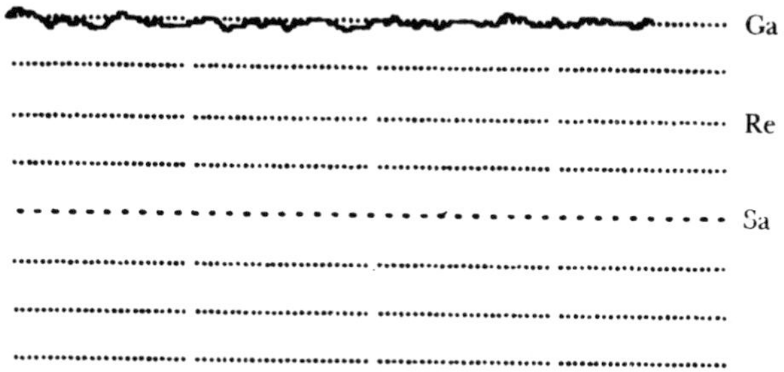

Ga
Re
Sa

Graph 45. Prabha Atre with aa

Ga
Re
Sa

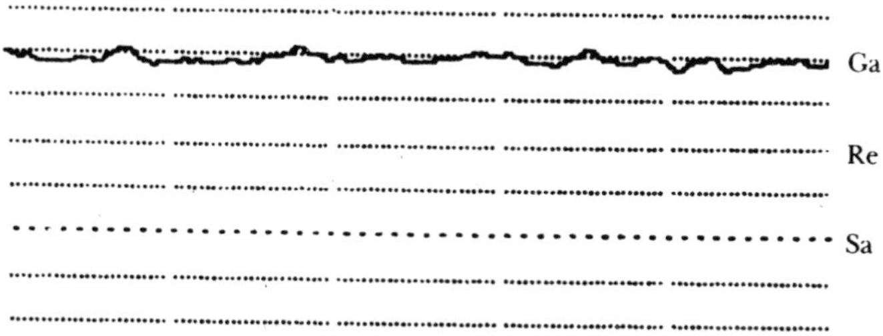

Graph 46. Amir Khan with a

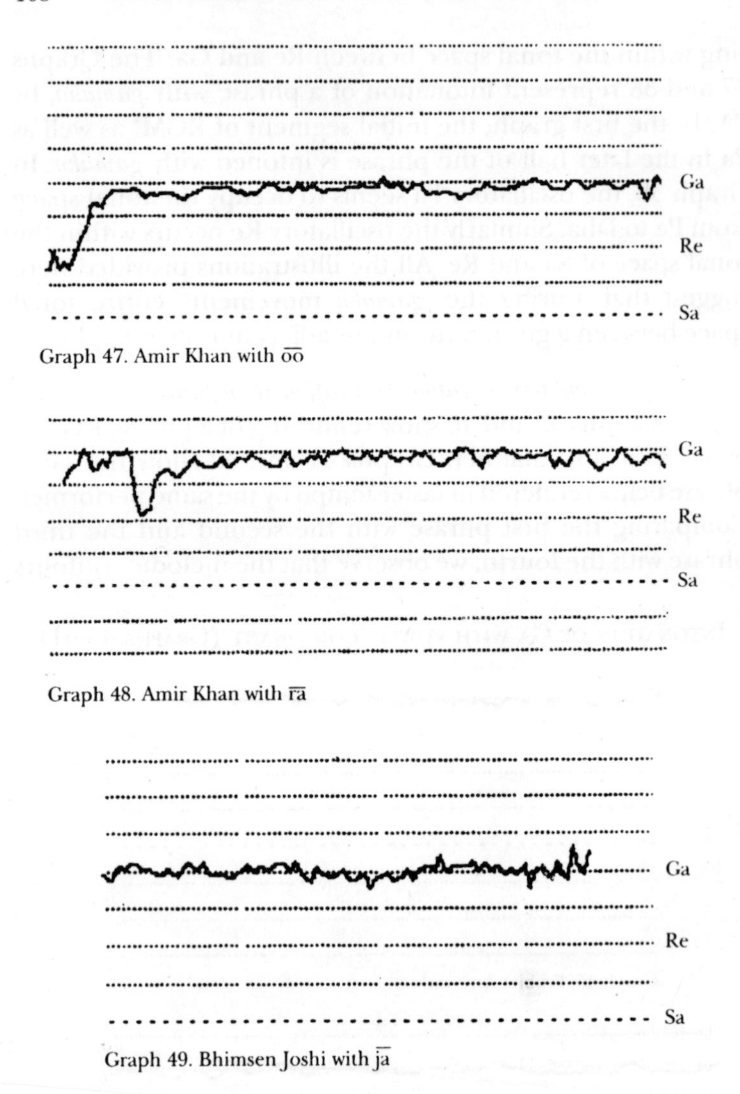

Graph 47. Amir Khan with o͞o

Graph 48. Amir Khan with r͞a

Graph 49. Bhimsen Joshi with j͞a

representing these renderings reveal subtle differences in intonation. Although these differences are appreciated aurally, their physical identification remains elusive. Nonetheless, all the four melodic graphs do show remarkable consistency which probably makes the finer differences less noticeable. The consistency of shapes and relatively small pitch deviations

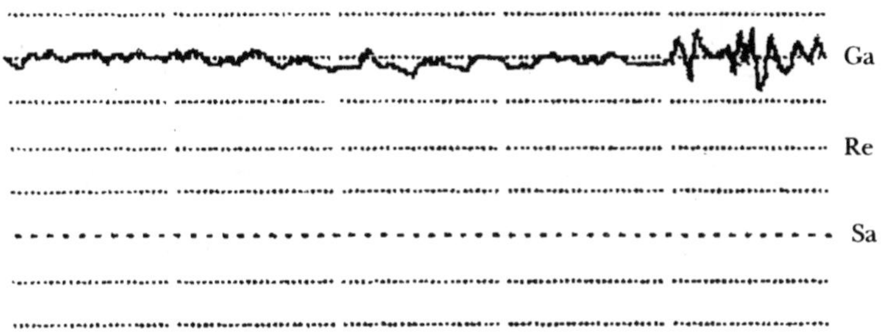

Ga

Re

Sa

Graph 50. Bhimsen Joshi with n̄e

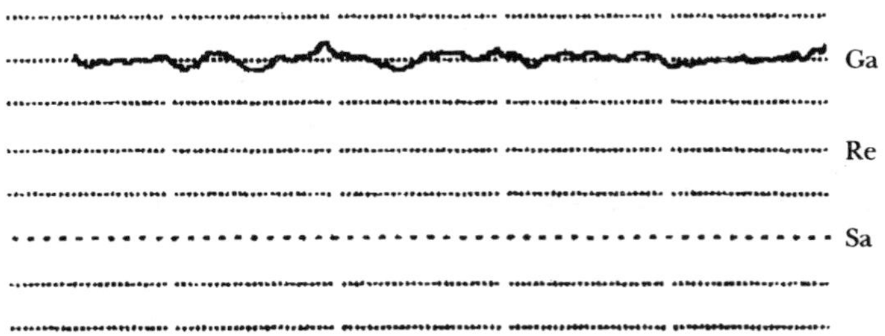

Ga

Re

Sa

Graph 51. Bhimsen Joshi with ēe

on these graphs indicate a very high degree of stability of voice production. This observation gains further support by Graphs 43 and 44 showing intonation of the same phrase RGM#P by AM.

(j) *Effect of accompanying vowel/consonant*

In vocal music, the textual element incorporating vowels and consonants is very significant. The syllables perform manifold functions such as carrying the musical notes, to bring variety in pronunciation, to build a rhythmic form and also to lend an emotional colour.[3] The following graphs illustrate influence of the accompanying syllables on the melody-line as well as that on the resultant pitch. The recording of PA was made under controlled conditions and one of the specification given was to use only āa for the complete performance. Hence all the intonations are accompanied by āa. Whereas, in case of AM and BJ, no such control was

INTONATION OF PA WITH VOWEL/CONSONANT

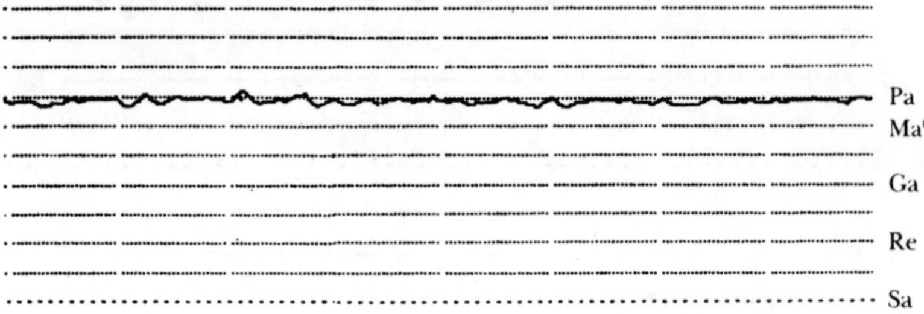

Pa
Ma#
Ga
Re
Sa

Graph 52. Amir Khan with a̅a̅

Pa
Ma#
Sa

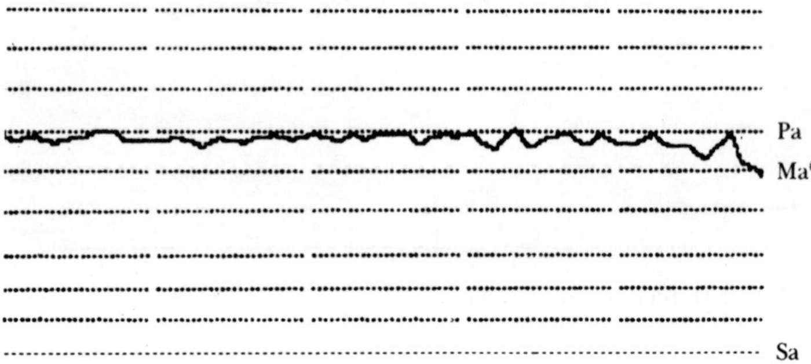

Graph 53. Amir Khan with j̅a̅

Re
Sa

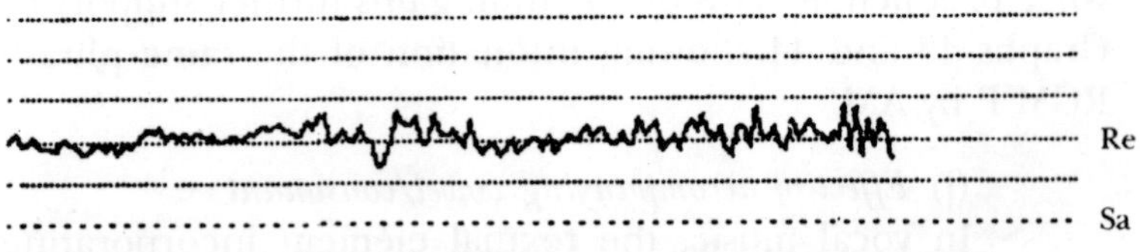

Graph 54. Bhimsen Joshi—Re with a̅a̅ followed by r

possible. Hence, their intonations are associated with syllables such as a, o̅o̅, r, r̅a̅, e̅e̅, a̅e̅, j̅a̅. Graph 45 shows intonation of Ga using a̅a̅ by PA while Graphs 46, 47 and 48 represent intonation of the same note by AM, using a, o̅o̅ and r̅a̅ respectively. For better comparison, Graphs 49, 50 and 51 showing intonation of the same note by BJ using j̅a̅, n̅e̅, e̅e̅ respectively, are provided. The melodic contours associated with the vowel sounds a̅a̅ and e̅e̅ appear to be smoother than those associated with n̅e̅ (a̅e̅) and o̅o̅. Further, the intonation accompanied by r̅a̅ appears to have the most deviant contour.

Graphs 52 and 53 indicate intonation of Pa by AM using a̅a̅ and j̅a̅ respectively. Both the melodic lines appear equally steady, except that in case of the second intonation with j̅a̅, pitch seems to have lowered. Intonation of Re by BJ using a̅a̅ and immediately followed by use of r can be seen in graph 54. The influence of these two syllables on the accompanied note is very evident from the melodic lines. Table 25 provides information about pitch of the same note intoned by same/different performer, using different consonants/vowels.

TABLE 25
Influence of consonant/vowel

Note	*Expected value in cents*	*Prabha Atre*		*Amir Khan*		*Bhimsen Joshi*	
		Consonant/ vowel used	*Pitch in cents*	*Consonant/ vowel used*	*Pitch in cents*	*Consonant/ vowel used*	*Pitch in cents*
Ga	386	a̅a̅	398	a	392	j̅a̅	412
				o̅o̅	376	e̅e̅	397
				r̅a̅	378	n̅e̅	384
						y̅e̅	380
Pa	702	a̅a̅	704	a̅a̅	684	a	705
				j̅a̅	684	n̅e̅	695
				e̅e̅	687	e̅e̅	699
						n̅a̅	702
						e	705
Re	204	a̅a̅	196	a	197	r	208
							214
				a̅e̅	197	a̅e̅	216
				t̅a̅	198	n̅a̅	212
				a̅a̅	206	a̅a̅	186

Observations pertaining to the melodic movement of the *raga* being performed (*Yaman*) by PA, BJ and AM

(a) In spite of the subjective variance regarding the tonal content of the individual phrases (introduced by the element of improvisation), the melodic centres through which the *raga* structure has been built by the performers show a striking similarity. The order of different melodic centres around which the *raga* structure was evolved and the manner in which these centres have been artistically exploited to weave the tonal fabric of the *raga*, is almost the same for all three performers. The principal melodic centres in the order of their manifestation are, Sa or C, Ga or E, Pa or G, Ni or B and Sa or C. The course adopted to unfold the potentials of each of these centres displays twofold approach. The central note of the given melodic centre is first approached with tonal designs incorporating the notes lower in pitch. This is followed by reaching the same desired centre with the higher notes. For instance, during the development of Pa or G by BJ, initially, phrases like

$\mathrm{P\text{-}P\text{-}P\text{-}M^{\#}P\text{-}M^{\#}GP\text{-}M^{\#}PM^{\#}grgm^{\#}P}$

are used indicating approach from lower end, while phrases like

$\mathrm{P\text{-}M^{\#}D^{dppm}P\text{-}RGM^{\#}D\ N^{d}P\text{-}\underset{\cdot}{N}M^{\#}N^{d}P}$

are suggestive of reaching Pa or G through higher notes. Similar approach is also noticed in the development of Ga or E by PA. The phrases like

$\mathrm{\underset{\cdot}{N}R\text{-}{}^{g}R^{g}RG\text{-}{}^{r}\underset{\cdot}{N}{}^{g}R^{g}\underset{\cdot}{N}G\text{-}{}^{r}\underset{\cdot}{N}\underset{\cdot}{N}G\text{-}{}^{ng}RG}$

show approach with lower notes, while phrases like

$\mathrm{\underset{\cdot}{N}{}^{g}R^{g}R^{p}M^{\#p}M^{\#}G\text{-}RGRGM^{\#p}M^{\#p}M^{\#}G\text{-}GRM^{\#p}M^{\#}G}$

$\mathrm{rgm^{\#p}PM^{\#p}M^{\#p}G\text{-}RGM^{\#p}PR\ RG}$

indicate reaching the note through higher notes. When the performer has explored the melodic possibilities for a given melodic nucleus, progression towards the next melodic centre is observed.

(b) In all the three performances, Sa or C and Pa or G are invariably absent in the ascending passages. Hence, the progression of the ascending melody is like ṆRGM#DN, M#DN, while Sa and Pa appear in the descending movements like M#DNDNDP-M#GR or PM#GRS.... However, ascending phrases terminating at Sa and Pa are observed, e.g., M#DNS or RGM#P, etc. Sometimes, in ending phrases like GPR-GS, Ma# is omitted (PA) while in a phrase like DS (AM) Ni is omitted. Certain phrases showing a tendency to temporarily avoid specific notes, are in fact indirect means of emphasizing those notes. They serve the aesthetic function of making the note invisible for a short while and then revealing it to heighten its effect.

(c) Melodic phrases that occurred in all the three performances are ḌṆ, ḌS, ḌṆḌSṆ, RḌṆ, RḌS, ṆR, ḌṆGR, ṆRG, RSṆḌ, ṆRM#G, RGM#P, M#DP, RGM#DM#G, MD#N, M#DNSN, RGM#DNDPM#RG, RS. Apart from these phrases, certain note combinations involving big leaps and often executed with a smooth glide, have been noticed. They are: ḌGRSṆ, ḌṆG, ṆM#G, M#N, M#SN, RM#G, RPM#G, PRS. Of these, NM# is a perfect fifth while NG and RP are perfect fourths. Thus their inclusion in the performance may be to intensify the consonant effect.

(d) Specific notes have been employed to support or balance the intonation of certain notes. The melodic centre of Ga in lower tetra-chord is juxtaposed by Ni in the upper tetra-chord. For the melodic development around Ni, Pa is used as a *nyasa-svara* or a resting note. Similarly, the inflection of long held Ni and Ma#, have often ended on Dha and Ga respectively. Furthermore, the phrases used to develop Ga are similar in structure with those used for exploring Ni, e.g. NRG, NRNG, RM#G, etc., balance the phrases like M#DN, M#DM#N, DSN.

Thus, in this chapter, results pertaining to pitch of individual notes, vocal inflections and melodic movements of *raga Yaman* obtained by analyzing performances of Prabha Atre, Bhimsen Joshi and Amir Khan have been discussed. Further, the observations pertaining to the pitch of individual

CHAPTER 6

Conclusions

In the present study, an attempt has been made to investigate the relationship between *raga* and *rasa*. An acoustical approach is employed to understand the contribution of factors such as intonation and melodic movement towards the aesthetic atmosphere resulting from a *raga*. For this purpose, an analysis of performances of *raga Yaman* rendered by Amir Khan, Bhimsen Joshi and Prabha Atre has been carried out using two independent pitch-analyzing systems. The complete process of investigation is reported in the preceding five chapters.

The chapter 1 deals with the emergence of the *raga-rasa* concept. Various details including the concept of *rasa*, its aesthetic relevance, the historical evolution of the *raga* concept, etc. are outlined.

In chapter 2, an exhaustive literature survey of various theories and viewpoints relating to *raga-rasa* that have been proposed by different Sanskrit scholars and musicologists in ancient as well as in medieval and modern times has been presented with essential details.

Chapter 3 presents a brief survey of the viewpoints of Western musicians, scholars and psychologists regarding the emotion resulting from music. These interpretations are compared with the parallel views expressed by Indian scholars. The comparison is presented in tabular form for a clear comprehension of similitude.

Chapter 4, entitled 'Approaches used to study *raga-rasa* in the acoustical perspective', provides details of the hypothesis, reasons for adopting an acoustical approach and details regarding the choice of particular *raga,* vocal music, performers, *alapa,* etc. along with an in-depth description of the two systems used for acoustical analysis, viz. 'MMA' and 'LVS'. Further, the experimental protocol and the methods adopted for measuring the pitch of individual notes, and the approaches used for studying the melodic movements of phrases are also presented.

Chapter 5 provides results obtained from the experimental investigations. The pitch information obtained using two independent systems, is presented in tabular form. The details of vocal inflections of steady notes, intonation with *meend* and various embellishments, etc. as well as the melodic movements of the *raga* performed are discussed along with the relevant melodic graphs.

Conclusions that can be drawn on the basis of the present investigation with respect to vocal inflections and melodic movements of the *raga* analyzed, are presented as follows:

1. The results pertaining to pitch-measurements of individual notes and the subsequent discussion suggest that during a given *raga* performance, the pitch values assumed for different notes are neither rigidly fixed nor randomly varying. In fact, the musicians do seem to conform to particular range of pitch values in a given *raga.* Besides a fair agreement in pitch values of individual notes (see Table 16), the adjacent intervals also show a good consistency in most cases (see Tables 17 and 18). In addition, the examination of intervals of adjacent notes for a given performer (individually) also reveals a good agreement between 'one-semitone' intervals (like M#a-Pa and Ni-Sa) and 'two-semitone' intervals (like Sa-Re, Re-Ga, Ga-Ma# and others). Further, the average values calculated for fifths (such as Sa-Pa, Re-Dha, Ga-Ni, etc.) also indicate a good consistency (see discussion for Tables 17 and 18). These results suggest that even though there are appreciable pitch differences for a specific note, every performer seems

to be balancing his/her individual intonation in a given context. The pitch values obtained by other scholars for the renderings of the same *raga* by two other performers are consistent with those obtained during the present investigation (see Table 23). However, a large number of such intonation studies involving different performers need to be undertaken for the same *raga*, in order to arrive at a confirmatory statement about the 'favoured' pitch positions of the notes (sustained notes). These positions might possibly suggest the tonal ranges assumed by notes of the *raga*. Depending upon the context and melodic treatment, the tonal range assumed by a given note in a particular *raga* can also be meaningfully interpreted with the help of the intonation study mentioned above.

2. Pitch values obtained for different performers using 'MMA' and 'LVS' show a good consistency, which indicates that the values are indeed reliable (see Tables 19, 20 and 21). The comparison between the actual pitch values of different performers and the theoretically calculated values also reveals a reasonably good correlation. However, the degree of correlation varied to some extent according to the performer. Such correlation was seen best for the intonations of Prabha Atre, slightly lower for Bhimsen Joshi and still lower for Amir Khan. This disparity in pitch values may perhaps be due to the presence of the accompanying instruments. The recording of Prabha Atre was made under controlled conditions and hence the influence due to accompanying instruments was avoided by eliminating them (only tanpura was allowed). Recordings of Bhimsen Joshi and Amir Khan being of live performances, interference from the accompanying instruments was unavoidable. The pitch analyzing systems used in these investigations are limited in their efficiency to discriminate between voice and other instruments like sarangi, tanpura, harmonium, tabla, etc. which follow

the voice closely. The observed differences between the actual and the theoretically calculated pitch values could be due to such limitations of the analyzing systems.

As these instruments are very much a part of an Indian musical performance, they cannot be eliminated. Therefore, during a performance, the voice should be recorded separately for envisaging the intonation details, so that the results will be more precise and the analysis, far simpler.

Commenting on the differences observed between MMA and LVS measurements which seem to be quite noticeable with the male voices, Dr. Bernard Bel[1] has opined that this can be partly due to the shortcoming of the fundamental pitch extractor used with MMA, assuming that identical melodic segments are used for comparison. He has suggested capturing the second harmonic of male voices in order to yield a clearer pitch line.[2] According to him, another explanation would be that the ear is more sensitive to pitch variations in the range and spectrum of female voices than those of male voices.

3. Despite the differences in the melodic movement of *raga Yaman* and *Marubihaga,* the pitch values assumed by individual notes in these two *ragas* are fairly consistent (see Table 24). In the light of the limited data involving the same performers being compared for the above *ragas,* it can be merely surmised that the tonal ranges assumed for different notes in these *ragas* may not be very different.
4. Pitch measurements of a sustained note indicate that, even the pitch of 'steady' part of a note is influenced by the preceding and following melodic context. The notes involved in 'attack' and 'decay' of a given note and the manner in which they are intoned, together play a decisive role in defining the tonal range for the 'steady' part of a sustained note. This is why a simple relation between melodic movement and intonation cannot be

prescribed. Also, until many occurrences of the same contexts by many different performers have been studied, no consistent relationship between context and tonal ranges can be postulated.

5. The descending movement follows a more linear path than the ascending progression. In addition, these movements are also influenced by the speed of rendering. During the faster intonation, attaining the desired pitch is far more direct and accurate as compared to that during the slower rendering of the same phrase.
6. Techniques such as the double intonation of a given note and the application of *andolan* at the end of a steady note are means for enhancing the aesthetic appeal of a note. Ornamental features such as *kan, murki, gamaka,* etc. induce a distinct colour to the intonation. Some of the subtle nuances that are elusive to aural perception, are revealed on the graphic contours analyzed in the present study. This certainly ascertains the significance of transcription in identifying the intonation characteristics of a particular performer. Frequency deviations observed for individual notes occurring singly or in phrases intoned with embellishments like *kan, murki, andolan, gamaka,* etc., imply that these deviations are aesthetically acceptable in the particular melodic contexts. It is interesting to note that aurally *andolan* is clearly perceived, even though the pitch variations involved are rather small. Part of the *andolan* effect might be explained by volume and timbral information. This is a typical case showing that more sophisticated analysis methods including techniques such as sonogram, wavelets, etc. are required.
7. A given phrase intoned by two different performers or by the same performer at different instances may differ considerably depending upon the subtle differences in treatment given to the phrase. These differences may be appreciated by the trained ear but their physical analysis will only be possible when more advanced faci-

lities are developed for studying certain characteristics of graphic contours such as the angle, the slope of contour at a particular point and so on. The striking similarity of the shapes and relatively small pitch deviations observed in these renditions indicate a very high degree of stability of voice production. It would be useful to compare these graphs with the ones obtained with untrained singers, or even singers trained in other systems of music.

8. Different vowels and consonants employed by the performers to intone different notes do influence the pitch contour. Audibly perceived steady notes accompanied by different syllables such as $\overline{\text{aa}}$, $\overline{\text{oo}}$, $\overline{\text{ee}}$, $\overline{\text{ae}}$, r, etc. showed variance in the melodic contours. The disparity might be due to the influence of vowel frequency upon the fundamental frequency of the note. By comparing the smoothness of melodic contours of different notes accompanied by various syllables, it may be inferred that vowels such as a and $\overline{\text{aa}}$ lead to stable intonations (low standard deviations from the mean pitch), whereas the use of semivowels such as r, $\overline{\text{ra}}$, etc. results in higher fluctuations in frequency of the note intoned. Considering the significance of textual element (incorporating these vowels/consonants) in vocal music (unlike instrumental music), the aforesaid frequency deviations may not only be within the aesthetic norms but may also contribute towards the total aesthetic effect.
9. In spite of the subjective elements involved in exploring the *raga,* all the three vocalists exhibited remarkable similarity in their adherence to the basic tenets governing the *raga* structure and delineation. Resemblances regarding the intonation details and the melodic movements observed in the performances of *raga Yaman* by three different vocalists suggest that a *raga*-performance is a 'rule based' and 'model based' phenomenon.

Outwardly, the structure of a *raga*-performance may seem to be impromptu but in reality, *raga* exposition is essentially governed by certain rules comprising its grammar and also by the model preconceived in the performer's mind, which results from his/her training, experience, imagination and skill. Further, the similarity of tonal configuration also suggests that the basic tenets comprising the rigid core structure of a *raga* remain unaltered in every performance irrespective of the performer, thus retaining the characteristic identity of the *raga*. The variant factors such as the element of improvisation and individual style of the singer, etc. operate at a peripheral level introducing an element of subjectivity into the performance and yet leaving the core structure of the *raga* undisturbed. In fact, these factors prove useful in enhancing the aesthetic content by way of lending an individual colour to the total performance.

The similarity of tonal configuration consisting of intonation and melodic movement makes it possible to correlate the tonal configuration of the *raga* with the unique character of the *raga* and consequently to the aesthetic atmosphere or the *'gestalt'* or the *rasa* projected through the *raga*.

Today, an attempt has been made to study the aesthetic concept of *rasa* which was put forth nearly 2000 years ago. Such an endeavour made in the context of contemporary music, is not without limitations. The aim of the present investigation has not been to provide normative results that could be applied to obtain definite equations involving a particular *raga* and a specific *rasa*. However, it has been directed towards identifying the similarity of 'tonal configuration' involving elements such as intonation and melodic movement, that have been traditionally accepted as factors influencing the aesthetic process of *rasa*.

To enable quantification of the subjective parameters in music, an analytical approach was adopted which involved computers. Continuous personal involvement for aural judgments lent an inter-subjectivity to the entire process. Further, it is realized that music being an abstract art capable of eliciting psycho-physiological responses, its complete quantification is neither possible nor warranted. This problem is best described by P. Kugel, "trying to characterize all musical cognition in terms of computations alone, is a bit like trying to paint all landscapes without using green."

The present study is largely based on interpreting the melodic graphs that provide visual representations of music. Ideally, the graphs should reflect our perception. However, since the ear averages pitch perceptions, the melodic lines appear smoother to our ears than to our eyes. Besides, these graphs represent only a fundamental tone devoid of harmonics while evaluation at the aural level is of a complex tone rich in harmonics. Although the graphs could be modified (smoother or more deviant), in the light of present knowledge about the pitch-perception which is very subjective in nature, the degree of resolution adopted in the graphic system of MMA seems optimum for melodic representation. The graphic details elucidate extremely subtle nuances of music which may not be aurally distinguished, but which may well be influencing our perception and appreciation of music.

This study supports the hypothesis that intonation in Indian classical music (vocal) reveals a certain plasticity. The formulations such as "neither rigidly fixed nor randomly varying" as reported in the conclusions can be further strengthened by providing specifications of tonal range assumed by a given note in various situations of melodic context and treatment. Firstly, such a codification in terms of pitch alone is impossible, especially in the case of embellishments involving intricate movements. Secondly, a large number of performances will have to be analyzed so as to accurately define the plasticity of intonation. Nonetheless, until such a time, 'agreement with variation' often mentioned in this study, cannot be viewed as a 'contradiction'.

The present study is one among the very few efforts which are based on the analysis of realized material, i.e. the actual *raga*-performance, for understanding the problem of *rasa* in Indian music. During the span of five years, only two aspects of *raga*-music (intonation and melodic movement) out of many that are known to influence the aesthetic process of *rasa* experience could be studied. The concluding statements pertaining to the *raga-rasa* relationship are therefore based on an examination of these two aspects only. In order to provide a complete picture of the complex problem of *rasa*, all the other aspects such as the tempo, form, text, etc., also need to be studied. The physical information obtained in the present study can be further consolidated by undertaking a multi-disciplinary approach involving psychological and physiological aspects of the *rasa*-experience. For this purpose modern techniques of encephelographs and imaging of brain-response to sound stimuli may prove useful. Of course, any project of this magnitude will require a large team of dedicated researchers.

Certain problems that have surfaced during this study could be investigated in future. The plasticity in the intonation suggests 'tonality' as an important topic to be studied. The codification of criteria like 'absolutely in tune' (*surila*), 'slightly out of tune' (*kansura*) and completely 'out of tune' (*besura*), etc. in terms of tonal-range can be a major area to be explored. The concept of 'tonality' being very much a culture-dependent issue, will have to be studied with the appropriate cultural and aesthetic considerations. Similarly, melodic shapes associated with different note-treatments such as *murki, gamaka*, etc. as well as intonations with vowels/consonants, etc. could be studied and characterized. However, in order to undertake such endeavours it is imperative that advanced technological facilities of electronic and computer systems should be developed, so that these endeavours can gain momentum. At present, since such facilities are not available, the analysis of a vocal performance of twenty minutes takes nearly six months!

I hope that this study has provided an acoustical approach that would give to the study of *raga-rasa* a new dimension, previously unexplored. The similarity of tonal configuration comprising the intonation of individual notes in a phrase and their melodic movements observed in the performance of a given *raga* by different performers, reveals that a *raga* has a potential to create a unique aesthetic atmosphere. Language being an inadequate medium, the precise nature of the above mentioned experience cannot possibly be captured by means of known verbal expressions. Nonetheless, the present endeavour provides reassurance that the principles inherent in a *raga* and their aesthetic capabilities are not mere theoretical facts but are a practical reality leading to a blissful experience—'*rasa*'.

References

1. Personal communication, January 1993.
2. Ibid.

Appendix 1

Raga-rasa as specified by Sharngadeva in *Sangita Ratnakara*

	Raga	Rasa
1.	*Shuddha-sadharita*	*Vira, Raudra*
2.	*Shadja-grama*	*Vira, Raudra, Adbhuta*
3.	*Shuddha-kaishika*	Ibid.
4.	*Bhinna-kaishikamadhyama*	*Raudra, Adbhuta, Daanavira*
5.	*Bhinnatan*	*Karuna*
6.	*Bhinna-kaishika*	*Raudra, Adbhuta, Daanavira*
7.	*Gauda-kaishikamadhyama*	*Bhayanaka, Vira*
8.	*Gauda-panchama*	*Bhayanaka, Bibhatsa, Vipralambha-shringara*
9.	*Gauda-kaishika*	*Karuna, Vira, Raudra, Adhbuta*
10.	*Kesar-shadava*	*Shanta, Shringara, Hasya*
11.	*Botta*	*Shringara, Hasya*
12.	*Malava-panchama*	*Hasya, Shringara*
13.	*Rupa-sadhara*	*Vira, Raudra, Adbhuta, Vira-karuna*
14.	*Shaka*	*Vira, Vira-hasya*
15.	*Bhamman-panchama*	*Vira, Raudra, Adbhuta*
16.	*Narta*	*Hasya, Shringara*
17.	*Shadja-kaishika*	*Vira, Raudra, Adbhuta*
18.	*Madhyama-grama*	*Hasya, Shringara*
19.	*Malava-kaishika*	*Vira, Raudra, Adbhuta, Vipralambha*
20.	*Shadava*	*Hasya, Shringara*

21. *Todi*	*Harsha*
22. *Bengala*	*Ananda*
23. *Binna-shadja*	*Bibhatsa, Bhayanaka*
24. *Bhinna-panchama*	*Bhayanaka, Bibhatsa*
25. *Varati*	*Shringara*
26. *Panchama-shadava*	*Vira, Raudra, Adbhuta*
27. *Gurjari*	*Shringara*
28. *Takka*	*Vira, Raudra, Adbhuta*
29. *Hindola*	*Sambhoga-shringara*
30. *Shuddha-kaishika-madhyama*	*Vira, Adbhuta, Raudra*
31. *Dhanasi*	*Vira*
32. *Revagupta*	*Vira, Adbhuta, Raudra*
33. *Desi*	*Karuna*
34. *Gandhara-panchama*	*Adbhuta, Hasya, Karuna, Vismaya*
35. *Kakubha*	*Karuna*
36. *Saveri*	*Karuna*
37. *Bhoga-vardhini*	*Vairagya*
38. *Velavali*	*Vipralambha-shringara*
39. *Naga-dhwani*	*Vira*
40. *Sauvira*	*Vira, Raudra, Adbhuta, Shanta*
41. *Varati (Batuki)*	*Shanta*
42. *Karnata-Bengala*	*Shringara*
43. *Devakriti*	*Vira*
44. *Kauntaki-varati*	*Rati*
45. *Saindhavi-varati*	*Shringara*
46. *Dravida-gurjari*	*Harsha*
47. *Bhuchchhi*	*Shringara*
48. *Khama-iti*	*Shringara*
49. *Ramakriti*	*Vira*
50. *Chevati*	*Hasya*
51. *Vallata*	*Shringara*
52. *Shuddha-panchama*	*Shringara, Hasya*
53. *Malhari*	*Shringara*
54. *Shriraga*	*Vira*
55. *Madhyama-shadava*	*Vira, Raudra, Adbhuta*

56. *Somaraga*	*Vira*
57. *Amra-panchama*	*Hasya, Adbhuta*
58. *Dvitiya-saurashtri*	*Karuna*
59. *Prathama-lalita*	*Vira*
60. *Prathama-saindhavi*	all *rasas*
61. *Dvitiya-gaudi*	*Viraha, Vira*
62. *Harshapuri*	*Harsha*
63. *Takka-kaishika*	*Bibhatsa, Bhayanaka*

Appendix 2

Emotional effects attached to *shruti* by R.L. Batra

Names of the shruti	*Emotional effect*
1. *Kshobhini*	arousing, energising, awakening
2. *Tivra*	keen feeling, loud
3. *Kumdavati*	bright irridiscent
4. *Manda*	apathetic, dull
5. *Chandovati*	peaceful, tranquil, orderly
6. *Dayavanti*	compassionate, pitiful
7. *Ranjani*	pleasurable, delightful
8. *Raktika*	devoted, charming, colourful
9. *Rudri*	serene, composed
10. *Krodhi*	angry, wrathful
11. *Vajrika*	immutable, determined unshakable
12. *Prasarini*	argumentative, elaborating
13. *Priti*	love, liking
14. *Marjani*	purifying
15. *Kshiti*	egoistic
16. *Rakta*	attachment, fondness, partiality
17. *Sandipini*	infatuation
18. *Alapini*	amorous
19. *Madni (Madanti)*	ardent, passionate, mad
20. *Rohini*	intense pleasure or pain
21. *Ramya*	beautiful, attractive
22. *Ugra*	formidable, grave, serious
23. *Kshobhini*	arousing, energising, awakening

Glossary

abhinaya	histrionics
acoustics	branch of physics which studies sound
Adbhuta	one of the nine *rasas* (aesthetic sentiment), evoking an experience of the marvel
alapa	improvisatory exposition of a *raga* in a slow tempo with or without the accompaniment of drums
alapti	the delineation of *raga* (in ancient text)
alpatva	rareness of a note
amplitude	maximum displacement of a particle of medium from the mean position
amsha	predominant note
ananda	a state of spiritual bliss
andolan	small oscillatory movement of notes
anubhava	consequents
anuvadi	assonant note
apanyasa	semi-final note
aroha	ascending series of notes
audava	pentatonic structure
avirbhava	straight forward display of the *raga*
avroha	descending series of notes
bahutva	profusion of a note
bandish	composition
bhava	aesthetic expression of a sentiment
Bhayanaka	one of the nine *rasas*, evoking an experience of horror

Bibhatsa	one of the nine *rasas*, it evokes an experience of odious
bola	words of the composition, often used for musical exposition in the form of *bola-alapa* or *bola-tana*
cent	1/1200th part of an octave
chromatic	either sharp or flat variety of a note
complex-wave	a wave representing mixture of fundamental and harmonics
desi-ragas	*ragas* independent of drama in ancient period
Dhaivata (*Dha*)	the sixth note
dhruva	*jati*-based vocal composition
diatonic	scale having two tetrachords of tone-tone-semitone and linked by a tone
frequency	number of vibrations per second of a sounding body
fundamental (frequency)	basic frequency of the sounding body (devoid of overtones)
gamaka	expansive oscillatory movements of notes, also used as a generic term to indicate embellishments
Gana	music included in drama
Gandhara (*Ga*)	the third note
gharana	a school of artistic tradition
giti	melody type of ancient period
graha	initial note
grama	parent scale of ancient period
grama-ragas	*ragas* associated with drama in ancient period
harmonics	overtones with frequency equal to integral multiple of the fundamental frequency
Hasya	one of the nine *rasas* evoking comic experience
heptatonic	scale with seven notes
janya-raga	*ragas* derived from *melas*
jati	ancient modal pattern

kan	slight touch of other notes
Karuna	one of the nine *rasas* evoking experience of pathos
kavya	poetry
khatka	ornamentation involving brisk movement of a few notes
khayal	a composition used in the contemporary north Indian vocal music
Komala (note)	flat
laya	tempo
LVS	computer program based on the principle of sub-harmonic summation
madhya	medium tempo
Madhyama (*Ma*)	the fourth note
mandra	lowest limit of the tonal range
meend	glide
mela	parent scale since medieval period
melogram	graphic representation of a melody
minitonagram	a mode available for measuring pitch, on MMA
MMA	Melodic Movement Analyser—computer set-up specially designed for the study of Indian music
murchhana	scales obtained by shifting of tonic
murki	fast ornamentation involving many *kans*
natya	art of stage
Nishada (*Ni*)	the seventh note
nritya	art of dance
nyasa	a note on which a melodic phrase can end
pakad	catch phrase of a *raga*
Panchama (*Pa*)	the fifth note
prabandha	musical compositions of ancient and medieval period
prachalita	commonly practised
raga	musical mode predominant in Indian classical music
raga-dhyana	contemplative verse associated with *raga*

ragini	mode similar to *raga* but assigned with feminine character
rasa	aesthetic delight
Raudra	one of the nine *rasas* evoking the experience of the furious
Rishabha (Re)	the second note
riyaz	practice
Sadava	hexatonic structure
sahitya	literature, text
samvadi	note in perfect fifth or fourth with the *vadi*
sanchari bhava	contributory or transitory emotion
sangita	art of music
sargam	solfa singing
Shadja (Sa)	the first note
Shanta	one of the nine *rasas* evoking experience of calm
Shilpa-shastra	art of image-making
Shringara	one of the nine *rasas* evoking experience of erotic love
shruti	microtonal variation
shruti-jati	class of microtones
shuddha	pure, natural
sine-wave	a wave representing pure tone devoid of harmonics
sitar	plucked instrument with frets
soma	plant yielding an intoxicating juice
sthayi bhava	basic emotion
sukta	hymn
sutra	aphorism
svara	musical note
tala	rhythm
taleem	training
tana	melodic passages rendered in an increased tempo
tanpura	plucked string instrument without frets serves as a drone instrument
tara	highest limit of the tonal range

tirobhava	melodic patterns which hide the essential characteristics of a *raga*
tivra	sharp note
tonagram	a histogram of pitch measurements over the melodic line of a musical piece
trishul	trident
vadi	sonant
vadya	musical instruments
vibhava	determinant, cause
vikrita	modified
Vira	one of the nine *rasas* evoking an experience of the heroic
vyabhichari bhava	emotional states transitory in nature

Bibliography

Adilshah II, Ibrahim, *Kitab-i-Nauras,* ed., Nirmala Joshi, Bharatiya Kala Kendra, New Delhi, 1956.

Ahobala, Pandit, *Sangita Parijata,* ed., Kalindji, third edn., Sangeet Karyalaya, Hathras, 1971.

Aristotle, *Aristotle on the Art of Poetry* with a Supplement *Aristotle on Music,* trans., S.H. Butcher, ed., Milton C. Nahm, The Liberal Arts Press, New York, 1948.

Atharvaveda, ed., Vishva Bandhu, Vishveshvaranand Vedic Research Institute, Hoshiarpur, 1960.

Atre, Prabha, *Svarali,* Manjul Prakashan, Pune, 1991.

Batra, Raibahaḍur R.L., *Science and Art of Indian Music,* Lion Press Publishers, Lahore, 1945.

Bel, Bernard, 'Beyond Levy's Intonation of Indian Music', *ISTAR Newsletter* 2, New Delhi, 1984.

—, 'Pitch Perception and Pitch Extraction in Melodic Music', *ISTAR Newsletter* 3-4, New Delhi, 1985.

—, and Arnold, James, 'A Scientific Study of North Indian Music', *NCPA Quarterly Journal* XII, 2-3, Bombay, 1983.

Bharata, *Natyashastra,* ed., Manmohan Ghosh, 2 vols., Manisha Granthalaya, Calcutta, 1967.

Bhatkhande, Vishnu, *Hindustani Sangita Paddhati,* vol. IV, sec. edn., Sangit Karyalaya, Hathras, 1970.

Brihadaranyakopanishad, ed., W. Pansikar, sixth edn., Nirnayasagar Press, Bombay, 1923.

Brihaspati, Kailashchandra, *Bharat ka Sangit Siddhanta,* Prakashan Shakha, Suchana Vibhag, Uttar Pradesh, 1959.

Child-Irvine, 'Aesthetics', *Handbook of Social Psychology*, third edn., Lindzey & Aronson, 1969.
Coker, Wilson, *Music and Meaning*, The Free Press, New York, 1973.
Copland, Aaron, 'A Modernist Defends Music', *New York Times Magazine*, Dec. 25, 1949.
Daljit Singh, *Invitation to Indian Music*, Classical Music Circle, Ludhiana, 1978.
Damodara, Pandit, *Sangita Darpana*, ed., V. Sastri, Saraswati Mahal Series, no. 34, Tanjore, 1952.
Deo, Pratap Singh, *Sangitasara*, Poona, 1912.
Deokavi, *Raga Ratnakara*, Nagari Pracharini Sabha, Benares, 1912.
Descartes, Rene, *Compendium of Music*, trans., W. Robert, American Institute of Musicology, Rome, 1961.
Deva, B. Chaitanya, *The Music of India: A Scientific Study*, Munshiram Manoharlal Publishers, New Delhi, 1981.
Ebeling, Klaus, *Ragamala Painting*, Kumar, Basel, 1973.
Gangoly, O.C., *Raga-s and Ragini-s*, Munshiram Manoharlal Publishers, New Delhi, 1989.
—, 'Origin and History of Some Important Indian Melodies', *Sangeet Natak* 5, Dec. 1956.
Gautam, M.R., *The Musical Heritage of India*, Abhinav Publications, New Delhi, 1980.
Hanslick, Edward, *The Beautiful in Music*, Bobb's Merrill Co. Inc., New York, 1957.
Harivallabha, *Sangita Darpana*, British Museum MS. (1710 Samvat).
Hermes, Dik, 'Measurement of Pitch by Subharmonic Summation', *Journal of Acoustical Society of America* 83(1), Jan. 1988.
Holroyde, Peggy, *Indian Music*, George Allen and Unwin, London, 1972.
Jacob, Arthur, *The New Penguin Dictionary of Music*, fourth edn., London, 1979.
Jaidev Singh, 'The Concept of Rasa,' *Aspects of Indian Music*,

Ministry of Information and Broadcasting, New Delhi, 1957.

Jairazbhoy, Nazir, and Stone, A., 'Intonation in Present-Day North Indian Classical Music', *Bulletin of the School of Oriental and African Studies* 26, 1963.

Jeans, James, *Science and Music,* Cambridge University Press, 1961.

Jog, K.P., 'Some Concepts in Ancient Indian Aesthetics', *Psychology of Music,* Sangeet Natak Academy, New Delhi, 1975.

Kapileshwari, Balkrishna, *Shruti-darshan,* Continental Prakashan, Pune, 1963.

Karnani, Chetan, *Listening to Hindustani Music,* New Delhi, Orient Longman, 1976.

Kaufmann, Walter, *The Raga-s of North India,* Oxford IBH Publishing Co., Calcutta, 1968.

Kelkar, Ashok, 'Understanding Music and the Scope for Psychological Probes', *Psychology of Music,* Sangeet Natak Academy, New Delhi, 1975.

Keller, Marcello, 'Some ethnomusicological considerations, about magic and therapeutic uses of music', *International Journal of Music Education,* no. 8, Berlin, 1986/2.

Langer, Susanne, *Philosophy in a New Key,* Mentor Books, New York, 1953.

Levy, Mark, *Intonation in North Indian Music,* Biblia Impex, New Delhi, 1982.

Lobo, Antsher, 'Multiple functions of *Vadi* and *Samvadi*', *Aspects of Indian Music,* Ministry of Information and Broadcasting, New Delhi, 1957.

Lochana Kavi, *Raga Tarangini,* ed., D.K. Joshi, Aryabhushan Press, Pune, 1918.

Matanga, *Brihaddeshi,* Trivandrum Sanskrit Series, vol. XCIV, Trivandrum, 1928; ed., Premlata Sharma, 2 vols., Indira Gandhi National Centre for the Arts, New Delhi, 1994.

Menon, Raghav, *The Sound of Indian Music,* Indian Book Co., New Delhi, 1976.

Meyer, Leonard, *Emotion and Meaning in Music*, Chicago, Chicago University Press, 1956.

Morgenstern, Sam, ed., *Composers on Music*, Pantheon, New York, 1956.

Mursell, James, *Psychology of Music*, W.W. Norton & Co., New York, 1937.

Nanyabhupala, *Bharatabhashya*, ed., C.P. Desai, Indira Kala Sangit Vishwavidyalaya, Khairagarh, 1961.

Narada, *Panchama-Sarasamhita*, ed., B. Singh, Manipuri Nartanalaya, Calcutta, 1984.

—, *Sangita Makaranda*, ed., L. Garg, Sangeet Karyalaya, Hathras, 1978.

—, *Chatvarimsatchata Raganirupanam*, ed., B.S. Sukhatankar, Bombay, 1914.

The New Encyclopaedia Britannica, Micropaedia, vol. 6, Encyclopaedia Britannica, Chicago, 1977.

Padhye, Prabhakar, 'Imagination weaves a rhythmic pattern of energy in art', *Psychology of Music*, Sangeet Natak Academy, New Delhi, 1975.

Parswadeva, *Sangita-samayasara*, Trivandrum Sanskrit Series, vol. 87, Trivandrum, 1925.

Patwardhan, Vinayak, *Raga-Vidnyan*, vol. III, sixth edn., S.R. Sardesai, Pune, 1960.

Pingle, Bhavanrao, *History of Indian Music*, Susil Gupta, Calcutta, 1962.

Plomp, R., *Aspects of Tone Sensation: A Psychological Study*, Academic Press, New York, 1976.

Podosky, Edward, *Music Therapy*, Philosophical Library, New York, 1954.

Popley, Herbert, *The Music of India*, YMCA Publishing House, Calcutta, 1950.

Prajnanananda, Swami, *Music of South-Asian Peoples*, Ramakrishna Vedanta Math, Calcutta, 1979.

Pratt, Carroll, *Meaning of Music: A Study of Psychological Aesthetics*, Johnson Reprint Corporation, New York, 1968.

Rajgopalan, K.R., and Chandrasekharan, M., 'Appeal of

Karnataka Music', *Studies in Musicology,* ed., R.C. Mehta, Baroda, 1983.

Rajopadhye, Vasant, *Sangitashastra,* published by the author, Bombay, 1959.

Rana Kumbha, *Sangitaraja,* eds., Telang and Pansikar, Nirnayasagar Press, Bombay, 1913.

Ranade, Ashok, 'Affective Analysis of North Indian *Ragas*', *Psychology of Music,* Sangeet Natak Academy, New Delhi, 1975.

Ranade, Ganesh H., *Hindustani Music: Its Physics and Aesthetics,* third edn., Popular Prakashan, Bombay, 1971.

Rao, Suvarnalata et al., 'A Study of Intonation in Hindustani Classical Music,' *Journal of Acoustical Society of India,* vol. XVII (3 & 4), Delhi, 1989.

Ratanjankar, Shrikrishna, 'Individual Notes and Specific *Rasas*', *Aspects of Indian Music,* Ministry of Information and Broadcasting, New Delhi, 1957.

Rath, Raghunath, *Natyamanorama,* Orissa Sahitya Academy, Bhubaneshwar, 1959.

Redlich, Hans, ed., *Mahler Symphony, no. 6, A Minor,* Ernst Eulenberg, London, 1968.

Revesz, *Introduction to Psychology of Music,* trans., G.I.C. de Courcy, Longmans Greens, London, 1953.

Rigveda Samhita, ed., S.D. Satavalekar, Swadhyaya Mandala, Aundh, 1959.

Sahukar, Mani, *The Appeal in Indian Music,* Reliance Publishing House, Delhi, 1986.

Seashore, Carl, *Psychology of Music,* sec. edn., Dover Publications, New York, 1967.

Shardatanay, *Bhavprakashan,* ed., B. Sandesara, Gaekwad's Oriental Series, Baroda, 1968.

Sharma, Premlata, 'Rasa Theory and Indian Music', *Sangeet Natak,* journal of Sangeet Natak Akademi, New Delhi, April-June 1970.

—, 'Raga and Rasa', *Report of Twelfth Congress of the International Musicological Society,* Berkeley, 1981.

Sharman,Gopal, *Filigree in Sound, Form and Content in Indian*

Music, Vikas Publications, New Delhi, 1970.
Sharngadeva, *Sangita Ratnakara,* trans., R.K. Shringy and Premlata Sharma, vols. I & II, Munshiram Manoharlal Publishers, New Delhi, 1991, 1996; trans., G. Tarlekar, Maharashtra Rajya Sahitya Sanskriti Mandal, Bombay, 1975.
Shubhankar, *Sangita Damodara,* ed., G. Sastri, and G. Mukhopadhyaya, Sanskrit College, Calcutta, 1960.
Somanatha, *Raga Vibodha,* ed. and trans., R. Aiyar, Madras, 1933.
Srikantha, *Rasa Kaumudi,* ed., A. Jani, Oriental Institute, Baroda, 1963.
Stravinsky, Igor, *Chronicles of My Life,* Victor Gollancz, London, 1936.
Strunk, Oliver, ed., *Source Readings in Music History,* New York, W.W. Norton & Co. Inc., 1950.
Swarup, Bishen, *Theory of Indian Music,* Swarup Brothers, Allahabad, 1950.
Tagore, Sourindra Mohun, *Sangita-sarasamgraha,* I.C. Bose & Co., Calcutta, 1875.
Taittiriya Upanishad, ed., W. Pansikar, sixth edn., Nirnayasagar Press, Bombay, 1923.
Tembe, Govind, '*Raga* and *Rasa*', *Aspects of Indian Music,* Ministry of Information and Broadcasting, New Delhi, 1957.
Thakur, Onkarnath, *Raga ane Rasa,* Baroda, 1952.
—, *Pranavbharati,* 1956.
—, *Sangitanjali,* vol. III, sec. edn., 1979.
Van der Meer, Wim, Personal Communication, 1990.
Vanarase, Shyamala, 'Conceptual Framework for Analysis of Aesthetic Behaviour', *Psychology of Music,* Sangeet Natak Academy, New Delhi, 1975.
Venkatmakhi, *Chaturdandiprakashika,* ed., S. Shastri et al., The Music Academy, Madras, 1934.
Vir, Ram Avatar, *Theory of Indian Music,* Pankaj Publications, New Delhi, 1980.
Ward, W., 'Subjective Musical Pitch', *Journal of Acoustical Society of America,* 1954.

Index